Michelle Peart

To the Left of Your North Star

Manifold Press

Published by Manifold Press

ISBN: 978-1-908312-69-3

Proof-reading and line editing: Two Marshmallows: twomarshmallows.net

Editor: Julie Bozza

Text: © Michelle Peart 2016
Cover image: © AstroStar: shutterstock.com
Cover design: © Michelle Peart 2016
E-book format: © Manifold Press 2016
Print format: © Julie Bozza 2016
Set in Adobe Garamond Pro

For further details of Manifold Press titles both in print and forthcoming: manifoldpress.co.uk

Dedication

With thanks to Lucy and Helen because without them
this book would still be in my head.

With thanks to Sonny and Julie for showing me the way.

With love to Robin and Holly for their encouragement.

Chapter One

The door to my crannog creaked open. "Time to go," the native boy said.

Finally, I could get the fuck off this godforsaken planet.

Unfortunately, my father had neglected to tell me that the best way to the Landing Plains, where his heap-of-junk spaceship waited, was by river. The blister-popping trek across what could've easily been anywhere on Earth to get to the Fire Glade had been bad enough. It had taken three long weeks to move my father's scientific team – a biologist, a geographer, a botanist, and an ecologist – plus all their equipment from his ship to the village. It struck me that the most boring people on Earth would fit well into the most boring place on Abaytor.

During that whole time, my father and I only exchanged a handful of words, as he either had his head stuck in a book or his nose in a flower studying bees. Being Herb's son was a lonely and unhappy life and sometimes a little frightening. When I was six, he left me alone by the side of a lake. He told me he wanted to look at a flower and that he'd be just a minute. I fell into the water and couldn't swim. A passer-by pulled me out. We never talked about it.

My father's studies had shown the bees were resistant to our insecticides and this, apparently, was significant. So I developed a loathing for the fuzzy little dive-bombers simply because they were important to my father.

Those three weeks were on top of the month-long journey in my father's scrapheap spaceship. There are only so many times you can *ooh* and *aah* at the billions of star clusters. Towards the end, with no privacy, no real heating, and fuck-all to do, it seemed preferable to open a hatch and float off into those stars. One particularly boring day, when I'd felt like I was asleep with my eyes open, I had pretended to spin the locking wheel and open a door, but nobody had noticed what I was doing so I'd sulked back to my corner.

Stepping out of the crannog, I pulled on a jumper. I wouldn't miss this odd copy of Earth, with its cold mornings and sweltering days, or the smoky fish smell that penetrated my expensive clothing or the goddamn cheerfulness of the locals, or … the list was endless.

The expedition would take six months, my father had said. I'd managed two and thought I'd done pretty well, considering the brain-numbing boredom and my strained relationship with him.

Slinging my bag on my back, I strolled to the end of the rickety walkway that connected the little thatched house on stilts to the land. Shielding my eyes from the sun, I looked for the native boy, Burn. He was by the river, stacking wooden crates on top of each other. The water shone copper in the morning light, with little flashes of golden fish darting in and out of the shallows. Jumping on to the sandy bank, I gave the crannog one last glance. Why would anybody build a house that creaks alarmingly when the river rages? As far as I was concerned, these people had a lot to learn.

Burn grinned and waved a long hand. I ignored his greeting, dropped my head, and stamped across the soft sand towards him. "Ready?" I muttered.

He pointed towards his creation bobbing eagerly at the water's edge. "It is all yours."

"Lovely." I placed a foot on to the wooden raft and immediately stepped back. "It wobbles." When Burn sniggered, I glared at him. "Seriously. It's not funny."

"I am not laughing, Ed."

"It's Ed*ward*, you dim-witted native."

Burn's cheery face was fucking annoying. "Do not worry, I built the raft myself, and it is safe."

I scowled and turned my attention from the native boy back to the floating piece of junk. It had a broad base of long thin logs knotted together with twine. On this was a triangular structure with a mucky brown canvas slung over it. The whole thing looked like a bad attempt at a Boy Scout's tent sitting upon a piece of flotsam.

"Here." Burn reached out. "If the raft scares you, I will hold your hand."

"Sod off, Burn. It doesn't." Yet there was a knot in my stomach as I marched on to the deck. The entire contraption reared like an unbroken horse. Swinging my arms in circles, I had to do a crazy dance to stay upright. I couldn't fall in; I still couldn't swim. My father never had the time to teach me and my mother hadn't liked to get her hair wet.

"Careful, you will have her over."

"Her?"

"Yes, I have called her *The Copper Queen*."

I turned to face the boy again, but as I moved, the raft listed to one side, unbalancing me. I hopped on one foot across the deck, and then with the grace of a new-born foal, I fell into the shallows. Little flashes of gold surrounded me. Batting them away, I stood up in the knee-deep water. "For fuck's sake." The water was as frigid as the morning air.

Burn stepped on to his *Queen* and she remained steady. "I was born on a raft like this." He reached out a long hand and dragged me aboard. "I grew up on the Copper River."

"How interesting." I sat on a barrel, took off my sneakers, tipped out the water, and glowered at my new transport. Burn's people were obsessed with living on or over water. The Copper River was a big deal to the people who lived in the Fire Glade. It was their road, their larder and one of their gods. I, on the other hand, hated it – the roar of the water scared me and the colour was worrying. I'd insisted on boiling my drinking water three times over. I heaved a sigh.

Stacked on the deck under the canvas tent were a bundle of furs, six wooden crates, and two honey barrels for seats. Heaped at my feet were a leather bag, containing what I presumed to be Burn's personal items, and my own rucksack – a top of the range Silverstrak with built-in music player.

Humming an out-of-key tune, Burn gestured towards his village. "Are you ready?"

Turning around, I glared at my father. This was entirely his fault – the raft, the annoying native boy, and the backwards planet. He was standing on the walkway of his crannog, fingers gripping the rail and towering above Naylor, the tribal elder. I liked Naylor; he had been kind to me during my stay in the Fire Glade and was one of the few people who'd even talk to the strange alien boy. He had a naughty sense of humour, which I loved, and many partners, which he loved. I had a feeling that most of the kids in the Glade were Naylor's.

Behind them, the scientific team stood in a huddled group. I knew they were desperate to get on with their studies and were only there to see me off through duty to my father. They never hid the fact that they didn't like me, referring to me in whispers as Herb's spoilt son.

My father's face was weathered and set in a permanent frown, and with his hunched posture, his whole body language said 'disappointed'. Nothing I did was good enough for him. I could get top grades in all my subjects at college but he'd grill me endlessly about the only subject I didn't excel in – science. Of course, this was his field of expertise: Herb Kemp, the renowned scientist and now famous explorer.

Discovering Abaytor had consumed him. He'd wanted me, his only child, to see what he saw and feel what he felt. Dragging me along on this trip was the result. He said it would be good for us, we could spend quality time together – but he was always too busy. To settle this, we were supposed to work together as father and son. I use the word 'work' loosely because I ended up spending most of my days under the shade of the cinnamon trees, holding the odd clipboard. My father's team hadn't trusted me with anything else. Neither had he.

For my father's sake, James, the ecologist and bad-tempered one, had *tried* with me. One day, he'd handed me a white plastic tray and an orange net on a long metal pole. "Get me some samples," he'd grumbled. He had no awareness of niceties. Maybe, over time, they'd been knocked out of him. It was clear he didn't like me and considered me a waste of space, but that was okay because the feelings were mutual.

I turned the tray over in my hand and stared at him through the net. "What samples?"

"For fuck's sake, Ed: river life."

"River life?" I repeated.

"Small fish, insects, larva, that kind of thing, I'm particularly interested to see if there are any river boatman."

"River boatman?" I was beginning to annoy even myself.

He'd clunked the clipboard against his forehead and said, "Just waggle the net around in the water, put the findings in the tray, and bring it back."

I'd felt about three years old as I sulked towards the water's edge. Within minutes, I'd lost the net. The current was stronger than it looked and had whipped it out of my hand. I put the tray down and tip-toed away, hoping James wasn't looking.

Another one to try with me was Blossom. She was the biologist and her main job was studying the bees. I thought she had a very apt name. She was fresh-faced, bouncy in all the right places, and laughed a lot. I liked her. She didn't like me.

I had to watch the bees and catalogue the most frequently visited plants, the time of the day, stuff like that. She said I could even sketch the flowers if I wanted. I didn't want. I fell asleep within the first half an hour of my watch and she never spoke to me again. It wasn't my fault. The bed in the crannog was lumpy and the never-ending sound of the water made me want to pee all the time.

The problem was, simply put, that I didn't feel what my father felt. In fact, I didn't give a fuck about the planet with its backwards and frankly sex-obsessed natives and total lack of creature comforts.

My father waved once in farewell. I ignored him, tilted my head back, and rolled my neck. My head hurt and the annoying native boy's humming added to the symphony of pain.

"Wave goodbye, Ed-ward." Burn's voice rang with merriment as he rammed his push pole into the sandy bank and heaved the *Copper Queen* into the twisting flow of the river. The raft jolted. I tumbled off the barrel, sprawled at Burn's feet and looked up into his stupid grinning face. He flashed his eyebrows and laughed. I so wanted to punch him, but I couldn't get off this hellhole of a planet without him.

I stood and my legs felt like pistons on the twisting deck. I looked back towards the Fire Glade. The sun was creeping up behind the Mountain of Bones, throwing long bronze reflections across the river's surface. For a second, I forgot about the annoying boy and saw the beauty my father had talked about my whole childhood. A tiny stab of regret prompted me to wave goodbye but he'd already turned towards the crannog. He entered the dwelling and never gave the river, or me, a second glance. Maybe the famous explorer Herb Kemp was glad to be free of his problem, the embarrassing son. I was no chip off the old block.

Burn steered towards the calmer waters at the edge of the river. My guide appeared to be around my age, perhaps younger. He had a wild look to him with large eyes, cheekbones sprayed with freckles and hair the colour of the river. Long limbed and scruffily dressed, like badly pegged washing, with a bow strung across his narrow frame and an intricate pendant swinging from his neck. I assumed that all the furs in the tent must be the result of his hunting skills.

Burn winked as I caught his eye.

I curled my fists – fighting was always my go-to reaction. Everyone in the Fire Glade appeared to be bedding everyone else. If the bloody native thought he could try it on with me, then he had another think coming. I don't do, and never will do, boys.

A look crossed Burn's face as he showed me his open palms. "Lighten up, Ed."

"It's Ed-*ward*." I sagged and gestured across the horizon. "What do you *do* on *Abaytor*? Why is it called that anyway?"

"Abaytor means second in our language, so that was the word your father chose. We call it Heras."

Typical. Earthlings conquer and rename, whether it's a tiny island in the middle of the ocean or a whole bloody planet.

Burn jabbed the pole into a shallow reed bed and shoved in the opposite direction. "I look after the bees. The ones your father and his companions have come to study."

"A beekeeper?" I gave Burn a pitying look. He clearly didn't aim high up the career ladder. I, on the other hand, was after the job of my father's best friend – chief executive officer of the Westcoast Bank.

"Well, I suppose. They are rare gold-tipped bees only found in the Mountain of Bones. Their honey has healing qualities not found anywhere else on Abaytor or –"

Zoning out, I stared at my wet feet. I missed my friends; they'd agree with me that my situation was pants and I had every right to complain. And my bloody mobile wouldn't work; this godforsaken planet hadn't invented the radio yet, never mind the telephone.

"What do you do, Ed, when you are not accompanying your father on his trips?"

I ignored him.

"Edward?"

Good God, the boy was persistent. "I don't *do* anything and I don't make a habit of accompanying him."

"What is it like having a famous father? I understand he is well known on your planet."

Fighting an urge to push Burn overboard, I said, "It's just peachy," before muttering, "My father's not paying you to ask questions, just to take me to the Landing Plains."

"Your father is not paying me at all."

"You're doing this for free? You're mad." Never do anything for nothing, is what my father taught me. Oh, and never let your left hand know what your right is doing. I still don't know what that means.

"Having now made your acquaintance, I think I probably am mad." Burn smiled and rammed the pole into a nearby bank.

"Why do you speak without using contractions?"

"Contract … what?"

Why the hell did I ask that question? I was in no mood for conversation. I sighed and said, "You say do not instead of don't or I am instead of I'm."

"I have never heard of don't or I'm, but I understand when you use them."

Unwilling to continue the conversation, I turned my attention towards the river. The raft had increased its pace in the tumbling flow. I shoved my fingers under the rim of a barrel. Not that it made much difference to my stability.

The landscape changed around us. The mountains shrank from imposing and sharp into forest-covered hummocks, and by the side of the river stood gnarly barked trees with umbrella canopies that cast creepy shadows. A dank smell filled my nostrils and there was a metal taste in the air.

I looked at my watch. It said eleven but that meant nothing. Abaytorians had no concept of time. It was so annoying. I liked the routine of lunchtime, teatime, or even bedtime.

"There is a waterstorm coming. If we are lucky, we will make the shelter of the Dragon Trees." Burn's arms swung in a wide arc as he wielded the pole. Fucking water again; if I'm not sleeping over it, or floating on it, I'm drenched by it.

Within half an hour, the sky turned from violet to charcoal and icy rain hit the raft with a loud *plipping* noise. I shivered and dived for the cover of the tent. Sitting cross-legged on a fur, I spied Burn through a crack in the canvas. Streams of water plastered his hair to his face and traced across his cheeks. The wind turned the river into an angry snake, making the *Copper Queen* pitch and yaw.

"Hang on," Burn shouted as the logs squealed and the raft reared. Out of control, I slithered under the canvas and past a wide-eyed kneeling Burn. Seconds later, I once again found myself in the copper water. But this time it wasn't the shallows, and this time I was afraid.

The cold hit me first; it stole my breath and froze my limbs. I spun in the water – rotating so fast that the raft was in view one second, then out of it the next. The river crashed around me, water filled my nose, and my heart moved from my chest and into my throat. By flapping my arms like a bird and pumping my legs as if I were climbing stairs, I managed to keep my head above the surface. Why hadn't my father taken the time to teach me to fucking swim properly? All I could do was the doggy paddle, and even that was debatable. Now I was going to die in a river on another planet and it would be totally his fault.

"Edward, *Edward!*" Burn's shouts hung above me.

Pushing my legs against the current kept my body in one position until the raft came into sight again. Burn was leaning over, aiming the push pole towards me. I lunged for it, forced my fingers around the end, and kicked the water as he heaved me in.

I sprawled across the deck with my designer clothes soaked and my hair feeling like a crow's nest. "Oh, I would give anything for a helicopter right now. Why hasn't this backward planet invented flight?"

Burn dropped to his knees by my side. He brought his face level with mine; I could smell something like lavender and feel his warm breath on my cheek, and whispered, "Do you think you could stay on board for the rest of the trip?"

I pushed him away.

That evening, we moored in a rocky inlet. I was wet and cold and Burn's shuffling around the raft was getting on my nerves. He prised open a random crate. I'm sure he'd forgotten what was in any of the six crates that cluttered our living space. In the days before our departure, I'd watched him build the raft with the enthusiasm of a prisoner building an escape tunnel. He'd loaded and unloaded the crates many times before finally deciding on what we needed for the trip. I never offered to help.

He upturned a crate and a grin spread on his freckly face as the contents spilled across the deck. I was hoping for supper; something like stuffed crust pepperoni pizza would have been welcome. Clearly, it wasn't Chicago Town's finest. Burn picked up some kind of dried meat strips tied together with twine, and a jar of red jelly that I hoped to God was jam. He unwrapped a cloth bundle to reveal what resembled budgie seed. Then he unpeeled another filthy package to uncover shrivelled fungi of various sizes. He swept his hand across the witches' pantry. "Supper," he proclaimed.

Dropping my head back, I groaned. I was either going to be drowned or starve to death before I reached the Landing Plains.

I awoke the next morning to a noise that sounded like half-snoring and half-banging. At first I thought it was Burn but he was gutting fish over the side of the raft. "What's that noise?"

"A white-eyed beater."

"Wide-eyed?"

"No. White. Their eyes contain so little pigment they are practically blind. Drumming their beaks on objects and reading the vibrations is the way they see."

"Oh." I didn't know what to do with that information.

"Did you sleep okay?"

"No. The logs stuck in my back, the furs were too prickly, and I don't believe you could lie still if your life depended on it." My body felt eighty years old as I crawled out of the tent.

"You will get used to it." Burn slung the fish guts into the copper water and they hit the surface with a sickening slap.

I had no intention of getting used to anything.

Burn passed me a wooden bowl with slivers of raw fish and leaves the colour of vomit.

"No, thanks."

He offered the food again. "You'll need your strength today."

"Why?"

"You will see."

I didn't take the bowl.

Standing on a ledge with red dust coating my bare feet, a wave of nausea swept over me. I closed one eye to block out the broiling mass of rapids in front of me and shouted above the thundering water. "Are you sure there's no other way around?"

"Quite," Burn yelled back.

A fat fly buzzed my nose. I batted it away and peered over my toes towards the river. A deep-sided canyon shaped like an egg timer forced the river to buck. The copper water had changed to dark brown with cream tips and twisted around huge boulders like a bubbling cauldron of frothy coffee. A white vapour hanging high above the surface smelt like wet earth.

"It is known as the Fifteen Flow Chasm," Burn offered.

"Flow?"

"It is our unit of measuring moving water."

"So don't tell me, we're fifteen *flows* down the river – how inventive." I scrubbed a hand across my face, spun on my heels, knotted my fingers behind my back, and paced a trail into the dust. That was, until I realised I was mirroring my father. He paced when he had a problem to sort. I stopped. As a child, I would try to catch my father's attention. I would be eager to tell him about the robot I'd built or my marks at school. He would bat me away like a fly – a simple flick of the wrist from him left a deep wound in me.

"Why don't we carry the raft over land?"

"The raft is too heavy. The two of us could not carry it through this terrain." Burn waved across the undulating rock-strewn land.

"Okay, you take the raft, I'll walk round."

Burn's shoulders slumped. "I would not make it alone."

I shook my head. "Okay, so what do we do?"

"We ride."

"We ride?"

"What is it your people say – on a wing and a prayer?"

"I *will* die."

"If the gods are with us, it is not today."

"Gods?"

"Yes, the god of the Rivers, and the god of Luck."

"Right." I rolled my eyes.

Burn caught the gesture. "You do not have gods?"

"Yes, but that's a completely different kettle of fish."

"Fish gods?"

I stalked off.

Secured on a small beach, the raft looked woefully inadequate for what we were about to undertake. We set about tying down everything that moved and Burn fastened two rope loops on to the front of the raft.

"Don't tell me, they're for me to hold on to," I said and prodded them with my toe.

"No, they are to put your feet in. I require you to paddle." Burn handed me a crude wooden oar.

"And you will be?"

"Standing at the back with the pole; I will use it to steer. Are you ready?"

"No."

"Do you want to go home?"

"Of course."

I'd never even seen a rapid before, never mind ridden one. Ramming my feet into the loops, I gripped the oar as if my life depended on it. I stared the beast in the face and felt like a sacrificial offering.

Burn shoved off and yelled, "Here we go –"

"Into the arse end of Hell," I finished.

At first, the *Copper Queen* was stable, but a sudden lurch pushed a cold fear up my spine and tightened my muscles.

"Paddle!" Burn shouted from the back.

Sticking my oar in, I strived to sweep through the water. It was hopeless. The oar spent a few seconds being useful and the rest of the time flailing in the air.

"Edward. *Paddle*!"

"I am fucking *paddling*!" I glanced back. Burn was using his pole to push off boulders that threatened the raft. His hair dripped from the mist and tendons were standing proud on his scrawny neck. I knelt, stuffed my ankles into the loops and facing backwards, I struck the oar into the copper water, and swept.

"Edward, you are paddling backwards!" Burn bellowed above the roar of the river.

Backwards, forwards, it was all the same. I changed direction.

The raft heaved to the left. I leaned to the right. The front lifted above a surge of white water, and for a second, we were airborne. My stomach flipped before we plunged into a depression between the waves. The jolt vibrated through me like a hammer striking a bell. "Holy cow!" We slammed into another wave. I lunged forward and clamped my hands on the edge of the deck. There was no way I was going back into the water.

The *Copper Queen* screeched as her logs jostled for freedom. A deluge of water swallowed me and, for a moment, I could have been anywhere. No up. No down. No time. No space. A few seconds of tranquillity before Burn screamed. Shaking the water from my eyes, I whirled round. He was gone. I searched the twisting waters, squeezing my eyes to focus and spinning my head in frantic movements. Nothing. My body tightened. He was fucking irritating but I was painfully aware I wouldn't survive the trip without him.

Panting, I shifted around, dug the oar in, and pulled. And pulled. With my heart knocking hard as flint against stone, I rode the *Copper Queen* through the twisting flow. Chucking my weight around allowed me to steer her around the larger boulders – but most of the time I just held on. The raft rode high like a piece of driftwood and the path she chose turned out to be the best. In the future, I would put down the oar and let the *Copper Queen* guide me.

The river calmed as quickly as it angered. I silently thanked God – any god – and stood up. Planting my feet on the deck and shielding my eyes from the sun, I scanned the water's edge and searched for Burn. My stomach rolled over. I had to find him.

His hair, still bright even though its owner was in the shadows of a rocky overhang, called to me like a distress beacon. With pole in hand, Burn waved and I expelled a long sigh. I was an only child with an absent father. I'd spent a lot of time in my own company and I didn't like it. A part of me was glad I didn't have to do this trip alone.

"Are your herd animals holy?" Burn said as he hopped on board.

"What?"

"Back there in the rapids you shouted 'holy cow'. Is that a god?"

I gritted my teeth and considered knocking him back into the water. "You are completely mad. No."

Burn examined me with his steady eyes then heaved off from the bank. "You did okay."

He coaxed the *Copper Queen* into a shale inlet under the shelter of a Dragon tree. Around us, the rusty-red walls curved in like an amphitheatre of rock leaving little room for the sky. The river was calmer here but still rumbled in protest as it bullied past. We surveyed the damage. Everything was soaking but still attached.

"We have the gods to thank for that."

There were no gods involved. It was sheer luck. I lay drying out in a narrow slice of sunlight. Should I have stayed with my maddening father and the stupid bees? My life wasn't in danger sitting under a tree in the Fire Glade. Maybe I could have just put my head down and got on with it?

I let my eyes wander past the high lip of the gorge. Little white puffs hung in a wedge of violet sky; it reminded me of a scarf my mother used to wear – she called it her seaside scarf because she'd worn it once on a rare family outing to the coast. We'd had homemade cheese scones and jam and my mother chided my father when he said jam only went with fruit scones.

She had just collapsed, they said, on her way to the Women's Fellowship. She'd been scheduled to talk on coping with fame in middle age. She'd complained about headaches for a couple of months. Migraines, the doctors had told her. Brain tumour, it turned out to be.

The fame that came to our family affected us all in different ways. My mother relished her new 'wife of the famous explorer, Herb' status. She stood taller. She spoke posher. She forgot about her only child.

Despite this, I still missed her.

Burn, humming a little tune, settled next to me causing me to tense as he shuffled up. I'd never liked people in my space. A soggy knee jammed into my side. I closed my eyes and hoped that the river, the raft, and the boy would just go away. When I opened them again, they were all still there. I pushed the knee back towards its owner. "You're so annoying. Has anyone told you that?"

"Yes. Many times."

A silence fell between us as the river slurped at the *Queen*.

Chapter Two

Herb stood outside his crannog and squinted into the early morning light. He scanned the copper water, and trailed the flow until it turned a corner. To his ire, much of Abaytor was like home. He had been expecting a radically different planet. After all his hard work and sacrifices, he deserved a radically different planet. And people. He had great affection for Naylor and his tribe, but if he was honest, he was expecting Greys, or the same basic shape but another colour. Even after three decades in the study of the sciences, the 'little grey alien' still infiltrated his brain.

One of his many sacrifices had been his relationship with his son. He'd tried to recover that by bringing Edward to Abaytor, involving him in his work and spending quality time with him. But from day one, Edward had shut him out. Herb admitted to himself that his work on Abaytor kept him so busy he may have ignored Edward more than he should have, but he'd thought the boy would've got stuck in like Herb had done when he was Edward's age. The only thing Edward seemed to enjoy was pissing him off with his sulking and deliberate mishandling of the simplest of tasks.

In spite of that, a week had passed since Edward had left the Fire Glade. Left *him*. It had been one of the worst weeks of Herb's life. He knew he'd failed his son and was worried the boy wouldn't survive if anything happened to his guide. And Herb wouldn't have blamed Burn for abandoning him: Edward was difficult at the best of times, and Herb dreaded hearing the news that the fearful Canibra tribe had taken his son or, worse still, that he'd drowned. He wished he'd taught him to swim but Abaytor had become his priority, even over his relationship with Edward. And yet, everything he was doing, the reason he was on Abaytor, was to save his son – and indeed all humanity. Of course, Edward had no idea. Herb could count on one hand the number of people who knew the awful secret that drove him. Though, he had thought after weeks of overhearing the conversations with his team, Edward would've started to ask questions. He never did.

A presence made Herb turn. The tribal elder, Naylor, was walking the flimsy walkway with silent footsteps. His brown face was shrivelled like a weathered conker, and his piercing eyes reminded Herb of good single malt. "Burn will keep him safe."

"Are you reading my mind, Naylor?" Herb looked down at the smaller man. Over the years of visiting Abaytor, he'd made a few friendships. Several visits to the Fire Glade had earned Naylor's trust and now they were firm friends. Sometimes in the lonely nights, they were more than that.

"Maybe." Naylor's eyes disappeared into smiling creases.

It had taken Herb many months to learn how to shut mind doors to prevent Naylor's telepathy from taking all his secrets. "You told me that Burn has hungered to see beyond the Fire Glade for many a summer. So why did you choose him to guide my son when he's never even left his village?"

"He is the only one who offered. Every traveller who passed through our village, Burn listened and learned from their tales of adventure and discovery. Do not worry."

That wasn't exactly the reassurance he was seeking. "But I am worried. I want to go after Edward."

"And do what exactly?"

Every paternal instinct in Herb screamed for him to follow. Nevertheless, he answered honestly. "I don't know."

"He will be long gone."

"Our craft is faster and didn't you say that Burn will take the opportunity to sightsee?"

"Yes."

"Okay, then." He'd faced a lot bigger hurdles in his quest for Abaytor. And while he had no idea what he would say to Edward when they caught up, he'd now made up his mind to go after the boy and nothing was going to stop him. His wife used to say he was like a dog with a rabbit when he got an idea in his head. "You will come with me, won't you, Naylor?"

The old man turned to view his friend. "What you hope will happen, will not happen. Yet, I will."

"Speaking in riddles again?" Herb rolled his eyes. He was never one for beating around the bush; he called a spade a spade and found Naylor's inclination towards flowery language grating. He strode off to begin preparations.

They loaded provisions into an inflatable cataraft that Herb had left behind on an earlier visit. He wished he'd left the boat at the Landing Plains; then he could have shoved Edward in and stopped him moaning about his feet. But they'd needed more samples, mostly botanical, that couldn't be carried by boat, and with the stakes so high the last thing he'd had on his mind was creature comforts.

The craft's silver pontoons reflected the water, and its red-and-white striped canopy buzzed against the neutral backcloth. Naylor bounced up and down on his inflatable seat with the water's flow. "What do you hope to achieve if we do catch the boys?"

Herb could see from his expression that he didn't find bouncing a pleasant experience. He shoved away from the bank. "A ceasefire."

The cataraft had a small diesel-powered motor. To keep pollution at a minimum, Herb planned to use it only for an hour a day. As Naylor clung to the shiny plastic sides, Herb push-poled the light boat away from the bank knowing that just this once, he'd side-lined his principles in favour of his son. He wished Edward understood that everything he was doing was really for him, for his survival on a planet that they'd all royally screwed up. And if push came to shove, if his team couldn't solve the greatest challenge to humanity's survival, then maybe, just maybe, Edward could find sanctuary here on Abaytor. All Herb wanted was for his only son to be safe.

The last sunny rays of the day clung to the horizon as they moored the cataraft and stared at the view in front of them. "Fifteen Flow Chasm," Naylor said.

"Looks – fun," Herb replied. "I can't imagine Edward was happy about going through that."

"Burn probably gave him no choice."

"That boy may do my son some good." Maybe Edward would see something he liked about the place.

"Burn is annoying but he has a certain attraction."

"Like someone else I know." Herb pushed off. "Are you ready?"

"I will pray for a good passage."

"You and your bloody gods." He was sure that Naylor must worship up to a hundred different gods. Herb didn't believe in any higher forces himself, but he secretly hoped Naylor's god of safe passage was with them.

Chapter Three

"The Temple of Anrad," Burn stated. "The house of the Haruspex."

"And they are?" I asked, but was not interested in the answer. I just wanted to go home, but Burn insisted on stopping every two bloody minutes to look at a flower, examine animal tracks, or now visit buildings. He was as bad as my father.

"Soothsayers. The chosen ones spend their nights studying the star nurseries and their days inscribing prophecies. The writings say that by the time they are eight, their path is selected."

Okay, I had to ask. "And the not-chosen ones?"

"They eke out a living farming on the steep barren land."

"Bum deal." I gave the temple a bare glance. Up on a high peak was a decrepit collection of pyramid structures, clinging to the mountainside like limpets. The evening sun reflecting off their pale walls made them appear ghostly and uninviting.

"All this stopping is annoying. Let's go." I stuck my hands in my pockets and made to leave.

"You live your life with your eyes shut, Edward. Come on." Burn started up the narrow path towards the temple.

This journey was getting beyond a joke. "You're so fucking irritating," I yelled after him.

"What does 'fucking' mean?" Burn called back as his copper hair and gangly limbs disappeared around a curve in the path.

I dropped my head back and groaned. The boy was *so* annoying. In my college, there were three groups: the sporty, driven types who burnt out by the time they were twenty-five; the cool clever types who never fulfilled their potential; and the brainbox geeks who were into sci-fi. And never will they mix. Ever. Burn would have been a brainbox geek. Of course, I was a cool kid.

The path was treacherous at best and lethal at worst. Some brave soul had carved narrow uneven steps in the rock face. Wooden stakes, forced into cracks, held a twine rail and my knuckles whitened painfully on the support as I made a mental note to keep my eyes fixed ahead. The rough rock dug into my thin-soled sandals as I took one step after another. Unsuitable footwear for the job, and I wished I hadn't changed, but Burn hadn't told me I would be mountaineering today. Of course, I could have waited for him on the *Queen*, but a small part of me was curious.

The path narrowed to a chair's width. The wind blew my hair into my eyes, my knees trembled, and my head swam. Ever since I'd been trapped on a broken Ferris wheel at the age of nine, I was afraid of heights. Burn seemed unaffected. I concentrated on him and not the abyss next to me. The steps disappeared, replaced by loose scree. One false step and even the sure-footed would be with Burn's gods.

"Burn, this is dangerous. One slip and you're dead," I complained. "One of my favourite books is about an invading army climbing a path just like this one to reach a fortress at the top. Half the men were lost to the sea below." I'd asked my father to read that book to me a dozen times. He never did. "If my father knew where you'd brought me, he'd have your guts."

Turning around with the ease of a mountain goat, Burn took a few steps and stood firm in my space. I clenched my fists as he scrubbed a hand across his face. "Edward, you may not know a lot of things, but you do know how to moan."

We breathed each other's air for a moment and I noticed a faint smell of soap. Where was he hiding soap? I hadn't washed for days. The wind hissed around the mountainside and a bird cried somewhere far off.

"Piss off." *Piss off,* was that all I could come up with?

"Would your father have my guts, Edward? Would he care?" Burn asked in a soft voice.

The last three words hit me like a blow to the stomach. No, he wouldn't.

"I swear when we get off this godforsaken mountainside, I'll … I'll –" My shoulders sagged and I nearly let go of the rail.

"You will what?"

My chest heaved with fear and with sadness as I stared out across the barren valley. How the hell did I get here? On another planet, breathing alien air, with my heart in my throat, and clinging to the side of a cliff like a fucking mountain goat? But Burn was right. Goddamn him. Pounding my spare fist against the rock face, I yelled out into the emptiness.

I was so tired of being me. My best friend, Jim, had two parents. His father worked as an accountant, his mother worked as a chemist, and he had a little sister who he adored. And the best part was that he had an oversexed girlfriend. I didn't want to be me, I wanted to be him.

Burn reached towards me but I swatted him away. He turned and I took a shaky step on the scree-slope. The edge of the path distorted as my vision blurred with tears.

The path widened – respite from the stomach-tightening ascent. I risked a glance up and wobbled at the sight. The Haruspex stood in a row on a bare ridge, poker straight and wearing lime-green robes with high yellow headdresses. They resembled tulips at a flower show.

"Be polite, Edward." Burn smiled at me then waved at the soothsayers.

"As if I'd be anything else," I grumbled. We reached the bluff and I took a step next to Burn.

Burn bowed and yanked me down with him. Wrenching away from him, I stood straight. Burn exchanged a long glance with presumably the leader of the group. He was a tall man with a long beard that had the middle section missing leaving a left side beard and a right. The other men had beards in the middle of their chins and not the sides. If one of these men had kissed the leader, they would have fit together like a beard jigsaw.

Burn and the tulip men exchanged no words as they turned to walk the last section of the path. Downwind of the soothsayers, a nauseating sweet smell hit me full on – *eau de tulip*. I coughed and made a face. Burn looked back, smiled, and winked. I swear, my father had purposely chosen the most irritating native in the village to take me home.

Stitched on to the side of the mountain was the first pyramid – balanced half on and half off a rock lip.

Sidling up to Burn, I muttered into his ear. "I'm not going in there. It's suicide."

"Scared?"

My father used to say, 'Are you scared, boy?' It always raised my hackles and prompted me to shout in response. Then he'd say I was quick to anger just like his own father. He'd had a very Victorian upbringing, speak when you're spoken to, that kind of thing. My mother had said that my grandfather hardly bothered with his son and certainly never played with him. My father would spend hours sitting on his hands in the cold cellar for the slightest mistake. And sometimes would be whacked around the legs with a leather belt for looking at grandfather in the wrong way. She'd also said she felt grandfather's childhood had been devoid of love and full of abuse and she didn't think he knew of any other way to parent his own son. My father never spoke about his childhood.

I shoved past Burn, strode through the triangle doorway, paused, squeezed my eyes shut then opened them again. It was not what I was expecting.

The structure had a square base with high sloping walls. On two sides, lines of triangular windows resembled teeth and gave the effect of being in the mouth of a monster. Multi-coloured tapestries hung from every spare wall space and elaborate rugs chequered the floor. One design dominated them both – a white human shape with a blue glow around its edges. Something about the image made me jittery.

The *eau de tulip* was strong and there was a chill, like when you stand in front of an open fridge. That was more than likely the reason for the fire in the centre. I followed the trail of smoke to the point in the ceiling, where it left through a gap. The soothsayers gathered around me, in silence, and Burn invaded my space.

"Why don't they speak?"

"They do verbalise but the Haruspex are telepaths. They prefer to communicate through thought transference."

I rounded on him. "Have they been reading my mind?"

"Yes. Whatever you do not have locked away will be readable."

"What the hell do you mean by locked away?"

"You mentally put your secrets and private thoughts behind a closed and locked door."

"Of course you do." I pressed my fingers to my forehead. The boy made my head hurt. Then a thought came and slugged me square on. "You haven't spoken to them yet."

"I have."

"Fucking hell."

"Edward, what does that mean?"

Ignoring his question, I demanded, "Are you a telepath?"

Burn took a step back. "Yes. That is how I learned your language."

I stared at him long and hard before jabbing my finger into his collarbone. "Have you been reading my mind?"

"I am not skilled enough to turn it on like that. It comes when I do not expect it, but I have been party to some information."

Taking a step into his space I snarled, "What *information*?"

A polite cough made us rotate as one. Wearing a jaded smile, the Haruspex leader said, *Join us,* without opening his mouth and nodded for us to sit.

"Burn, he's in my head."

"Relax, Edward."

The Haruspex and some newcomers wearing brown robes sat in a rough square around the fire. I slumped down between Burn and a young man about my age. He smiled at me – a warm genuine smile that lit his face. His relaxed manner and pleasant features reminded me of Jim. So, despite myself, I smiled back.

Let us weave hands, the leader said in silence.

With reluctance, I held Burn's hand and then the hand of the boy to my right. They dropped their heads as one. I peered out from under my overgrown fringe.

"This is nice." Burn squeezed my hand.

I scowled at him and fought an urge to run. This was way out of my comfort zone – strange people, a weird room and holdings hands with boys.

Edward, what you think you are seeking is not what you are seeking, the voice in my head said.

"What the hell does that mean?" I mumbled to anyone who was listening.

What you run from is what you need to run to.

What a load of codswallop. I yanked away from Burn's grip.

And we are sorry for your loss.

"What loss?"

You will grieve very soon.

"For who?"

That is not clear.

"So you're not that good, then." As a child, my mother would hold psychic evenings. I'd huddle on the stairs and eavesdrop on the wordy voice of the clairvoyant. To my young ears, it all sounded like a load of mumbo jumbo. As it did now. "Okay. What about Burn?"

Burn, you are running with happy abandonment.

"Lucky Burn."

And we are sorry. You will also grieve a loss.

"Lovely. I'm off."

"Edward?" Burn took my arm.

A lethal path, a man in my head, and prophesies of grief. I'd had enough.

Edward, it is coming, they all chorused.

I jumped with the many voices in my head and then pushed myself to my feet. "What the fuck are you talking about?"

Beware of the fog.

Beware of the fucking fog? Lovely. I marched out of the building.

"Edward." Burn's footsteps fell behind me.

"You are supposed to take me to the Landing Plains." I rounded on him. "I didn't ask for a sightseeing tour."

"You did not ask for it but it is what you need."

I pointed over his shoulder. "You sound like them."

"I promise I will get you to your ship. What are you rushing back for?"

"Normality."

"There is no such thing. Is it a girl?"

I shook my head.

"A boy, then?"

"No!" The blood pounded in my ears as I said, "You tell me, you've been rummaging around in my head."

"You have had no one dear to you since your mother died."

That was too close for comfort. Fucking alien head invader. I curled my fist, yelled and then ran past Burn towards the closest tree, brought my arm back – and then slumped to the ground with my head in my hands.

Burn hoisted me up.

"I was Chair of the boxing club for three years running," I said.

"A chair?"

"Never mind."

"And you hit trees?"

I sighed.

The Haruspex gathered in the doorway of the pyramid and wore expressions of pity as we took our leave.

"They did not predict that," Burn said.

"No." I waved with faked enthusiasm at the tulip men and then guided the boy in front of me. "You can go first, Burn. If I plunge to my death, I can take you with me." It was a joke, but I half meant it.

Chapter Four

Herb watched Naylor jog down the steep path. He'd been waiting several hours in the stuffy air and had almost decided to climb after him. But his knees, worn out from years of manual work, would not have allowed such a steep ascent. With the help of his ship design team, he'd built his *Wave Rider*; he knew every screw, every wire, and every circuit board. And during the long cold nights, his knees took a pounding from kneeling on freezing floors and climbing endless ladders.

Herb mused over the fact that he knew how to build a spaceship but he didn't know how to tell his son he loved him. He'd tried many times but the words had stuck in his throat. He blamed his father's hostility, his mother's tendency to turn the other cheek, his childhood, but deep down he knew it was his own fault.

"The Haruspex ... saw the boys ... a few days ago," Naylor said out loud and pulling deep breaths between words.

"Are they sure it was them?"

"A grumpy alien boy and a grinning native."

Relief flooded him. Edward was still alive and okay; at least he was until a few days ago. "Yes, that's them. I bet Edward loved that visit."

"They said he was – resistant – to their telepathy."

"He's getting a lot more than he bargained for on this trip." Edward was narrow-minded, believing his way was the only way. Herb was positive Burn would upset Edward's apple cart and he hoped that would do his son some good. He had tried and failed to expand Edward's interests by exposing him to his own hopes and dreams. Edward had blocked him at every turn. Maybe the young native could broaden Edward's horizons in a way he couldn't.

That evening around the campfire, Herb swallowed some dried gristle and tried his best not to bring it back up. In the days before Abaytor consumed him, he'd travelled far. While backpacking the Road of Bones in Russia, he'd suffered loneliness, trench foot and prehistoric-sized mosquitos. But he'd also experienced kindness from the locals, and had often been offered a bed for the night or a meal.

One of the first things he'd learnt was that it was rude to refuse food, no matter how bad it was. Once, in a Mongolian yurt, he'd eaten goat's testicles, straight off the animal and into the frying pan. It had taken a great deal of will power not to projectile vomit the smooth globes back at the goat.

Herb looked at his plate. "What are we eating?"

Naylor, half-lit in the fire light, smiled and said, "Bear."

"Bear?"

"Well, our version of your bear which we call ursus."

It had taken Herb a while to get used to the locals' abilities to telepathically translate his English words. "It is an acquired taste." He put his empty plate down and shook his head. "You'd think after all this time I'd be used to the cuisine on this planet."

"How many times have you visited Heras now?"

Herb held up a hand and dropped one finger at a time as he counted. "Five."

"Who gave you the – what do you call it – money?"

"An establishment called a bank funded me. A good friend is the boss of a large one." His meeting in the plush Westcoast Bank offices of Thomas Smyth had been prickly. Surrounded by stony-faced government officials and scientists, he'd tasted fear in the room. An ecologist had flapped a handful of papers in his face and yelled, "There's no doubt any more. The bees will die out worldwide within the next few years. And we all know what that means for humans on this planet." He'd sat heavily as if to make a point. "Starvation and war," he'd concluded and chucked the report on to the desk.

Then an official with halitosis had barked, "The fate of billions of people, indeed civilization as we know it, rests on your shoulders."

Herb had carried that weight heavily, especially after the parting words of the bad-breathed official: "You don't want people slaughtering one another over food do you, Mr Kemp?" Of course he fucking didn't. Numbskull. And so he'd agreed to the mass importation of Abaytor's bees, which were somehow immune to the pesticides wiping out Earth's bees.

His friend, Thomas, had grabbed his arm on the way out of the office and pulled him into a corner. "You know you're not alone?" he'd whispered. Herb had released himself from his grip and nodded yes.

"Governments like to keep the kind of secrets that everyone knows about. There are other crews heading to Abaytor as we speak. They want the glory of bringing home the bees."

He'd had an urge to shout in Thomas' face, *It's my planet, they're my bees, how fucking dare they?* But he'd resisted and looked at the floor instead.

"They're ruthless, Herb. They'll have no interest in keeping Abaytor pollution-free or fitting in with your precious natives."

"They've got to get there first." Herb had turned from his friend and got the hell out of Westcoast Bank.

"I always look forward to your visits." Naylor interjected his thoughts.

Herb smiled at him. "I cause you nothing but problems, old friend." The villagers had not taken kindly to his initial visits. Even today, many people still regarded him with suspicion and fear. He'd had to deal with many a village gathering to reassure them he meant no harm.

"Yes, it is true. You take over my village, eat all our food, and bother the bees."

"And don't forget I also frighten your children."

Naylor laughed. "I do not know why we put up with you."

"I will be forever in your debt."

"That thought is pleasing." He winked.

The fire died and the warmth with it, so they moved into the cataraft that bobbed at the water's edge.

"How long until we catch up with the boys?" Herb inquired.

"A day." Naylor settled against a bouncy side and knotted his fingers behind his head.

"I'm sorry to drag you away from your people and your duties to chase down my son."

Naylor patted the space next to him and indicated for Herb to sit. "I am having a – what is that word – holiday."

Herb plonked next to him and pulled his knees up against the chill as

Naylor draped an arm around his shoulders. He enjoyed Naylor's attentions much more than the many women he'd been with. When he was instructed to import Abaytor's bees, his first thought wasn't saving the world's food production, it was for Naylor and the buzz in the pit of his stomach when he saw him.

"I was the first alien on Abaytor. How did you know you could telepathically translate?"

"The Ancients instructed me in a dream."

"The Ancients?"

"Yes."

He didn't want to ask. If he was honest, he was weary of Naylor's gods, but he felt compelled to, so he sighed and said, "Okay, so who are the Ancients?"

"They are the true gods who control all the minor gods and therefore all life on Heras."

Herb's scientist brain had never grasped the concept of unseen deities so he decided not to pursue it any further. "Okay," he said in a very definite *conversation's finished* kind of way.

Naylor slipped his arm further until his outspread fingers rested over Herb's heart.

"Are all Abaytorians so – forward?" He twisted in Naylor's embrace to face him.

"Yes."

"Well then, Edward will be having a super time." His son didn't tolerate anything he deemed as different to himself. In an effort to kick free from his suffocating upbringing, Herb had embraced a diverse life. He nestled in Naylor's warmth. "So, am I alive?"

Naylor counted. "One, two, three, one, two, three. Your heart is beating fast."

"Yes, I can feel it. To be honest, I'm surprised I haven't keeled over from a heart attack."

"You put too much pressure on yourself."

"Other people do that for me, Naylor." The silence that followed and the sway of the cataraft lulled him into a much-needed sleep.

Kicking the office door shut, he leant against it, and closed his eyes. The only sounds were the distant chatter of tellers' voices, the whir of the air conditioning, and his heart beating in his throat.

A passing secretary said, "Mr Kemp, are you okay? You look pale."

He smiled falsely. "Yes. I'm fine." He wasn't. He felt as if he were carrying a bomb that was due to explode at any moment. The fate of food production was in his hands. There was no choice: he had to deliver Abaytor's bees to Earth.

The garishly-patterned carpet at his feet swirled and morphed into filthy bare floorboards. He looked up to find he was standing knee deep in rubble with a grey sky above. Around him, people were huddled in the ruins, some staring at him, some crying on the shoulders of others. A man ran past, battered, bloodied, and holding a rifle. He stopped when he saw Herb and took three long strides until he was inches from his face. He smelt of death. "Mr Kemp," he yelled, "this is your fucking fault, your fault, your fault —"

He woke screaming.

Chapter Five

The cellar under the ruins radiated cold; every stone face added to the reflective chill. The odour of damp fused with a heady scent of lavender. I shoved the heavy ironbound door closed behind us.

A lone wall torch cast dancing shadows across racks of spears and shelves of storage jars. Somebody was still using this place. To one side, tarnished helmets sat above breastplates, with gloves resting in front. They looked like waiting knights with front row seats for the performance.

"This way." Burn took my wrist and led me into the gloom towards the far end of the cellar. I stumbled over the unknown with the eagerness of his lead. In the shadowy depths, he stopped. His breath was hot on my cheek as he stepped into my space. My heart clattered out a beat and my muscles tensed. He looked astonishing — his hair shone like polished bronze in the torchlight and a faint pink blush stained his cheeks.

Burn forced me backwards against the damp stones. His weight expelled the air from my lungs in one long groan. He smelt of fresh air and exuded cold. He knitted his fingers with mine and brought my hands above my head. A soft warm mouth met mine. I took a sharp breath.

"Relax, Edward." His words vibrated on my lips.

For the first time in a long time, I did as someone told me. I relaxed into him. Burn felt the shift in my body and rumbled a low sound. He kissed along my jawline and down my neck; I tilted my head to allow him access.

What … was I doing? None of this made any sense, but God have mercy, it felt so good.

Burn's hands wandered over my shirt, twiddled the hem, slipped under the fabric, and across my goose-bumped skin. I shuddered under his caress.

I sat up, arrow straight, and blinked at the mucky canvas above my head. My heart drummed in my ears as I drew ragged breaths, scanned my body, and examined my hands. I couldn't think straight. What was that? Where am I?

"Edward?" Burn sat on the edge of the *Queen* with his feet dangling in the copper water. "I think you were dreaming. You were moaning a lot." He looked mischievous, like he'd been caught with his hands down his pants.

A shudder rushed down my spine. "More like a nightmare," I grumbled and crawled out of the tent. I'd never had those thoughts for Burn, or any man.

Shielding my eyes from the sun, I turned a full circle. High above, a bird squealed and I winced at the sound. I was sure the wildlife on Abaytor was happier than on Earth because they were bloody louder.

The raft was ambling her way through a narrow cutting in an arid bottomland where the water seemed to be the only thing moving. A dusty surface littered with rocks and shrivelled free-roaming bushes lay to each side of the river. Tall plants, definitely from the cactus family, stood like lone sentries with their thick branches angled into a high five position. I needed spurs on my boots, a lasso around my waist, and a horse. Burn was by my side in two strides. In return, I took two steps away.

"Was it a nice dream?" Burn's eyes sparkled. He knew something. Goddamn brain invader.

There was no way I was going to tell him. "What was in the soup you made last night?"

"Herbs, grains and —" He paused, as if scratching around to recall.

"None of your funky mushrooms?"

"No. Why?" He beamed at me.

"No reason." Stretching my stiff limbs, I scoured the deck for my bag. The need to re-acquaint myself with the familiar was strong. My tablet still had enough battery life to view the photos. On our first day on the river, I'd shown Burn the digital photos. His face had lit with wonder. Then, to his distress, I took a picture of him. He muttered for the rest of the day about stealing his essence. This gave me great satisfaction – he'd invaded my brain, I'd captured his soul.

I stooped, but before I could pick up my Silverstrak, Burn placed his hand on my shoulder. Spinning around, I swatted it away. Burn recoiled in surprise and we held each other's gaze for a long moment.

"You made me jump." It was a lie; I didn't want him touching me.

"I am sorry."

Shaking my head, I turned away from him.

"Edward," he said nervously.

"What?"

"We have company."

The dream slipped from my mind as a lapping sound filled the quiet morning. I sensed that my father was minutes from my side.

"Son." The throaty voice was unmistakable.

My first thought was not for my father and the inevitable discord that his presence brought, but for his boat. The cataraft was bigger and far superior to the *Queen*; it would have made our journey easier and faster. Along with half of the Fire Glade, my father had watched Burn build his raft. So why hadn't he offered us the use of his craft?

Naylor sat at the back of the craft, silent and unmoving. When I allowed my eyes to settle on my father, he was staring at me, his face expressionless.

I drew a slow and steady breath. "Father."

Herb drew his craft alongside the *Copper Queen*. "Permission to come aboard," he chipped.

Resisting an urge to stamp my foot, I said, "No."

"Yes, of course, Mr Kemp," Burn said.

I shot him a look that could have killed, then turned my attention back to my father. "Why are you here?"

"I thought we could clear the air before you left." He didn't attempt to board, he just looked at his feet and coughed. "Your mother wouldn't have wanted us to be at odds like this."

"Don't bring my mother into this." The words came out in a rush as I tightened my fists.

Herb sighed as if the weight of the past few years were almost too much to bear. "I just wanted to know you were okay."

Where had this out-of-character concern come from? I glared at him. "I'm fine. You can go now."

Burn reached out his hand to my father. "Break the fast with us."

"I said no, Burn," I spat.

"I heard you, Edward." Burn tugged my father aboard the *Queen*. My father's boots on my turf did not sit well and that surprised me, considering the raft wasn't mine. Burn turned his attention to Naylor and reached out to him. The old man stood and, with lightness beyond his years, hopped aboard unassisted. I passed Naylor a honey barrel and kicked the other one in my father's direction.

A hot breeze combed my hair and the same bird cried in the distance. My father glanced around. "A curlew," he said. "We had them near the river behind our house, before they built those damned apartments. Do you remember, Edward?"

"It might not be," I replied. "Just because it sounds like a curlew, doesn't make it a curlew."

My father gave me an incredulous stare and to my surprise, he actually agreed with me. "Yes, you're right. We really are going to have to get Biology to come up with some other names once they've finished DNA sampling."

I gave myself a virtual pat on the back. "Why can't you use their native names?"

My father didn't reply and, along with Naylor, we sat in an uncomfortable silence as Burn, wearing an apron that looked like it'd been tie-dyed in the seventies, made us breakfast.

"Where the hell did you get an apron from?"

"My bag."

"Necessary equipment?"

"Oh, yes," he replied and hummed the same annoying tune.

"Don't you know any other tune?"

"No. I do not."

How can he only know one tune? Nobody only knows one tune. And why was he wearing a bloody apron? Exasperated, I kicked a crate across the deck. "You see what you've subjected me to," I moaned. "He's a fucking numbskull."

Herb stood and took a few paces towards me. "Edward, don't swear."

Lifting my chin, I glowered at him through half closed eyes. "Why not?"

"You were taught manners, my boy."

"*You* didn't teach me *fucking* anything."

My father's chest heaved as he glanced in Naylor's direction. The tribal elder held his look for a moment before shaking his head slightly and examining his fingers. I wasn't normally intuitive but the gaze between my father and Naylor implied more than friendship. An image of the two of them entwined in the dead of night with deep breathing being the only sounds, popped into my head. I shook it off, screwed up my face, and hoped to God I was wrong.

"I didn't come here to argue with you, boy." My father turned on his heels, shifted a honey barrel closer to Naylor, and plonked himself down. I fucking hated it when he called me boy.

Burn served dry biscuits with honey and strange berries – a possible source of my weird dreams. He put the witches' potion, which he said was tea, on a small raised fire to boil. We ate in silence with unsaid words brewing as steadily as Burn's concoction.

In the end, my father spoke first. "Come back," he said, his tone almost deferential, "and we'll try again."

"Try what again?" I knew what; I was being pedantic and perhaps unfair.

"To be in each other's company. I'd like us to find some common ground and if we can't do that on another planet, where else can we?" He flicked a smile.

I crossed my arms. "How long did it take you to locate us?"

"A few days."

"A few days! Good grief, it's taken us over a week to reach this point."

"If you decide you can't hack it with me –" my father tipped his head towards his cataraft "– you can always take her to the Landing Plains."

Scowling at his boat I said, "Where were you hiding that?"

He examined his fingers. "I brought it on a previous trip to Abaytor."

"And you didn't think it might be useful for us to use?"

"I thought you'd have more, um, fun on the raft. I know I would have."

"I'm not you."

"I know that, Edward."

"Not interested," I said and walked away from him. But there was something in me that wanted to reconcile with my father. He was my

35

only family. I'd stormed away from the Fire Glade bubbling with resentment towards him. He'd dragged me away from all I knew, to spend six months on a planet I hated. Before I left, we couldn't even exchange two words without arguing. Maybe – I could try harder this time.

"Edward." Burn stood in front of me and leaned forward. I leaned back. "I think it is a good idea." The wind blew stray hair into his bright eyes and there was something about him I couldn't pinpoint.

"Have you been talking to Naylor?" I asked. The two Abaytorians had not exchanged words, but I'd seen their furtive telepathic glances. A pink blush stained Burn's cheeks bringing back memories of the dream.

"Yes," he said.

"And what have you been saying?"

"That you should go back. Your father has offered a truce. You should take it."

I viewed my father. A smile lit his face and then dropped as soon as it came, as if being happy was difficult for him. My mother used to say he was frightened of being happy in case it was taken away from him. I didn't know what that meant but I felt it had something to do with Grandfather.

"What about the *Queen*?" My concern for the pile of driftwood was surprising.

"Edward, she would not make it back from the Landing Plains. She cannot travel against the current. I was going to trek home. We can leave her here for now."

It hadn't entered my head to wonder how Burn would get home. I sighed, "Okay, I'll go back."

My father stood, put his arms out, paused, and then reached to shake my hand instead. "I'm pleased, son."

We fastened the *Copper Queen* in a sandy inlet and piled what belongings we had into the cataraft. I had a sudden thought and turned to Burn. "You're coming back with us, right?" Burn's view had never occurred to me and, I noted, he never offered it.

"I am not ready to go home yet, but you need to repair your relationship with your father. You are lucky to have one. So I will come with you."

Burn's parents had died when he was young. They were killed in a river rafting accident when he was ten, so he was left to fend for himself. I found it surprising that he appeared so well rounded; I probably would've ended up in a reform school for naughty boys.

I stepped off the *Queen* and on to the cataraft.

That night, with my father's craft rising and falling with the water, I settled back and watched the darkening sky; deep purple with black edges and a billion billion stars clustered into nursery groups. To one side, in a vast empty area, a large star shone brightly in the darkness. I knew that was home. It appeared so small and insignificant and it made me feel lost and alone.

My father and I had said little to each other since I'd agreed to return with him. Either the presence of others had subdued our conversations, or we didn't know what to say.

In the morning, while Burn and Naylor were hunting, I sat with him under the shade of an umbrella tree. He removed his jacket and hooked it skew-whiff from a low branch. Folded pieces of paper wafted to the ground. Picking one up, I flicked the yellowing square over in my hands. "Why do you keep these news clippings after all these years? There's been plenty of water under the bridge since then." I read the newspaper piece aloud:

"Extract from the City Gazette. Dated 2015. Mad scientist Herb Kemp —" I nodded in agreement "— visits Abaytor for a fifth time. On his fortieth birthday, the famous explorer, who achieved his dream of proving the existence of a parallel Earth last year, landed for a fifth time on its surface. He discovered the new planet, which had been in permanent eclipse behind a dying star, a decade ago. His custom-built ship, the *Wave Rider*, made the forty-day journey with his flight control team and a few minor hitches. Reports are now suggesting that the civilisation is five hundred years behind us. In a direct quote, Herb states, 'The natives can learn from our mistakes and keep their beautiful planet unspoilt.' He intends to impact Abaytor as little as possible, and except for a few key personnel, has no intention of taking space tourists any time soon."

My father silently took the clipping from my hands, and like he was handling a rare treasure, placed the scattered papers back into his jacket pocket.

"You know, space tourists will pay off the debts," I said.

"It's fine."

"I know it's not. How much do you owe the Westcoast bank?"

"I've lost count. Millions probably. Anyway, it's not about the money I owe any more."

"It's not?"

"No." He kicked the dirt.

"What, then?" I was actually having a frank conversation with my father. And it didn't include the word fuck.

"Bees. The pollinators on Abaytor have a different constitution and our studies show that they're resistant to insecticides. The government wants me to bring some back to replace the Earth bees."

"Which government? Why? What for?"

He stood and smiled down at me. "Our government. It could be the answer to Earth's dwindling bee population. Bees are very important to our food production."

"You don't talk about your work to me." I pushed up to join him.

"No, I guess I don't." He nodded and strolled away. I ran after him and opened my mouth to speak, but the moment had gone and we walked the rest of the way in silence.

The next few days passed in a blur of tussling for personal space on the cataraft. When we weren't aboard, we were carrying the light craft and its contents around the trickier parts of the river. I spent little time alone with my father, even after our brief connection, preferring instead to seek Burn's company. This didn't bode well for any future father and son reconciliation.

On the evening of the last night, Naylor produced the local firewater called mash. It was yellow with a luminescence that was worrying. With care, he poured three and a half measures into four little wooden chalices. At seventeen, Burn was handed the half measure. At eighteen, I was allowed a full measure. This pleased me. I made sure Burn could see my full measure as I raised it in salute and winked.

"Be careful, Edward, it has a kick that corrodes your eyelashes," my father said.

I didn't want him telling me how to handle my drink so I also tipped my cup in his direction before necking the mash in one. Bad mistake. The liquid burnt a line through my body until it set fire to my stomach. I gagged and struggled for breath. My father laughed and downed the firewater. He screwed up his face and held out his chalice for more. Naylor duly re-filled the cup with a warning that two was enough. My father drank his second and rested against the inflatable sides. "Whoa, that's good stuff, Naylor," he said, his words bumping into each other. He looked at me. "I'm glad you will come back," he slurred, "maybe you will learn something."

"What the *hell* is that supposed to mean?" I placed my hot and fuzzy head in my hands.

"Since you flunked college, you've not done much have you? You've had the world, actually two worlds, at your feet, but you chose to be a drop out."

"If you'd been any kind of father then maybe I would have chosen a different path," I hurled back.

My father lowered his head and appeared to shrink. "I gave you –" he burped, "the freedom to be who you wanted to be, do whatever you wanted to do. I never told you when to speak, what to think or who to be friends with."

What the fuck was he on about? "I needed guidance, Father. And I needed time, *your* time." I stormed off the cataraft with my heart pounding in my ears and blinking away the tears. With no thought about where I was heading, I stamped up a dusty mound to the side of the river, reached a low flat rock, and plonked myself down. The night air was heavy with summer's heat. Jabbing a stick into the red dust at my feet, I glared at Burn wandering up the hill towards me. I knew he'd follow me. He dropped quietly by my side. We sat in silence for a moment, carving up the dirt and listening to the chirrup of the crickets or whatever the hell they were on this planet.

"They say sober words are spoken through drunken ones." Burn carved a figure in the dirt and then another one holding hands with the first.

I frowned at the drawing. "I don't know my father. It's like he's played the famous explorer for so long he's even forgotten himself." Dropping my head, I said to the ground, "Before Abaytor consumed him, he was busy with his dream, but you could see ideas sparking in his eyes. That light seems to have gone."

"Then help him find himself, and you, again."

On the river below, the cataraft bobbed in the twilight. My father spread diagonally across the deck, presumably passed out. I knotted my fingers behind my head and lay back. My eyes, heavy with sleep and the effects of mash, closed.

A spindly arm reached out and long fingers connected with my forehead. My body stiffened as hot waves pulsed through me. Burn screamed. I passed out.

And opened my eyes to a blur of grey. Tremors quaked through my body and my head throbbed. Where was I? My fingers felt a hard edge running parallel to my side. I walked them up and over my head and blinked to clear my vision. What the hell? Lying flat in a see-through box all I could see were wires with round connectors pulsing with blue light.

I banged my fists against the lid and shouted. No reply. I cleaned a window in the grotty glass. Above me, there was nothing but a rocky ceiling and shadows. What did they want with me? Where was Burn? Had he succumbed to the same fate? In the nerve-jangling silence, I took a deep breath, and then another. At least I was alive. For now.

I awoke dripping with sweat. Burn was asleep at my side. My neck felt impossibly hot and the compulsion to run was strong.

Chapter Six

The Fire Glade looked the same, even smelt the same: a sickly whiff of honey in the air from the hundreds of hives dotted around the Mountain. Burn's dilapidated crannog, leaning alarmingly, stood apart from the rest.

The walkways to the crannogs were not the safest structures I'd ever seen, but Burn's was practically lethal. I stepped over a gap in the planks. "Burn, are you sure we're not gonna end up in the water?"

"Sure." A note in his voice said he wasn't.

The inside of the house was dim and sparsely furnished with a bed, a three-legged table, and a chair. The building creaked and groaned with the slightest puff of breeze and smelt like an old people's home. A single shirt, mucky at the collar and ripped at the hem, hung from a nail. Burn had nothing. My room, with its revolving bed and home cinema was, in comparison, embarrassing.

"Nice," I said and offered him a smile.

"Liar," he replied.

I drew a squiggle in the dust on the table. "You need a woman's touch."

Burn moved so close I could hear his breathing above the water lapping at the stilts of the house. "Or a man's …"

I supposed so, equality and all that. Picking up a solitary book, I blew away a thin film of sand and opened it on a random page. Hand-scribbled interconnecting lines and circles spread across the text. I raised an eyebrow at Burn who took the book, cleared his throat, and read aloud. "'I, for one, would follow you into the mouth of Nether,' the loyal knight said. 'Into the mouth of Nether it is,' the King replied and raised his sword. With his battered army behind him, the weary King stumbled forward."

"You read sword and sorcery?" That surprised me. "I have all the Martin Stanza books at home, including a rare first edition. In fact, I have this book."

Burn gave me a blank look before stating, "It *is* your book; your father gave it to me on his last visit."

"Oh, I'll send you more. On the next ship," I said in a sudden flush of generosity. "Not the first edition though," I added.

"You are kind, Edward. Please sit and I will make tea."

I couldn't face any more of Burn's tea. "Why don't you show me your bees?" Placing my hand on his shoulder, I guided him back out of the house.

The process of reconciliation with my father was making me anxious, and I was fully aware of my selfish use of Burn's company to avoid him. The trip back to the Fire Glade was not exactly harmonious. What if it didn't work out and I was left angry and hurt? Again.

The track was steep and rock-strewn but wide enough to walk two abreast. Burn sauntered with his hands deep in his pockets and his eyes lowered. I walked a step behind with my fingers knotted behind my back, like my grandfather had.

"Do you have a girlfriend, Burn?" The question formed and was out there before my brain engaged.

He stopped and considered me. "No. No girlfriend."

I hesitated. Could I ask him the next question? "A boyfriend then?" I blurted as if it was rude.

"No. No boyfriend, either." He took a step into my space and smelled like cut grass after the rain. "Are you offering, Edward?" he whispered.

"No. I'm not!" I took three steps back and my face flushed hot. My mind raced – was I offering? Those dreams I'd been having of late, did they mean I was offering?

Burn laughed and slapped me across the back. "It will be dusk soon and we do not want to be on the Mountain of Bones when the light goes."

"Why is it called that?"

"We lay out our wrapped dead in its creases."

A shudder vibrated through my shoulders. "Surely you mean bury?"

"No. Hollows in the rock face become their final resting place."

"Yuck. That's disgusting." My Earth-brain knew we buried sealed coffins out of sight to help us banish the memories. My father cremated my mother and threw her ashes to the wind until she vanished from my life completely. I often wondered if she would have chosen that method of disposal.

"To you, maybe." Burn placed his hand on my lower back and guided me up a narrow path to his right. I took a few quick steps to move away from him. Abaytorians were so fucking touchy-feely.

I can safely say that bees are bees wherever you are in the universe – small, furry, and buzzy. Burn's were no different. Boredom struck me within a few minutes of watching him fuss with the triangular beehives. He cooed and tutted at the tiny bodies until a loud sigh from me made him turn.

"Would you like to learn the art of beekeeping?"

"No, thanks." I yawned.

"Am I keeping you out of your bed, Edward?" He smiled and glanced skyward. "The light is going and precipitation is coming. We need to go."

"No one says precipitation, Burn. Say rain or weather."

"Rain," he repeated as we headed down the mountain.

At first, it was a light rain, or that is what I presumed it to be; it had become so dark I couldn't see beyond my nose. A fetid smell clung to my clammy clothes and there was a deathly silence. Fingers slid down my bare arm and interlaced with mine.

"Come," Burn's disembodied voice said.

Wrenching my hand away, I growled, "I don't need hand holding."

"I realise that, Edward." A ring of merriment in his tone raised my hackles and the desire to hit him was strong.

Soon, a heavy rain mugged us. Large drops nailed my exposed skin and stole my breath. A blue glow appeared with a sudden flick and hovered in front of me like a firefly. It revealed Burn's grinning face, and his hand clutching a silver horn-shaped vessel topped with a blue dancing flame.

"It seems you have everything in that magic bottomless bag," I said, referring to the small leather bag that Burn carried.

He ignored the comment. "We need shelter. There is a hollow near here."

"I hope it's not full of skeletons," I replied – to which Burn just shrugged.

Following the blue light I ducked under a large rock overhang and within ten paces, we'd reached the back wall. The glow, with Burn attached, sat down. My wet clothes rucked against my skin as I slid down the rock face to join him. We sat in silence listening to the *yuuuu* of the wind and the *dot dot dot* of the rain.

Burn broke the silence. "You cannot avoid your father for much longer."

"I know."

"You should go to see him at first light." Burn turned towards me and held the flame between us. Rivulets of water ran from his hair and traced the shape of his jawline. My cheeks coloured. I shrank back, away from the light, and away from the confusion that even Burn could have read on my face.

A fog slid into the hollow and rolled in little spirals against anything it touched. Burn gasped and his body stiffened next to me.

"Burn?" An uneasy feeling crawled up my back.

No answer.

"Burn," I repeated into the dark.

Still no answer.

I shook him and said his name again. My ears felt hot and my heart was beating in my throat. *Beware of the fog,* the Haruspex had said. What the fuck did they mean by that?

"Do not move, Edward. Stay as still as you can," Burn breathed.

Time slowed and I was still for only a moment but it felt like an eternity. Burn's body slackened and I relaxed with it.

"What the *hell* was that all about?" I asked in a loud whisper.

"Nothing."

"Nothing! You're scared."

"It was nothing, Edward. We should rest."

"The tulip men said beware of the fog. Why?"

"I do not know."

"Liar." I shuffled away from him. Sometimes I thought I'd figured him out, then other times it was clear he was alien.

I don't know what time I awoke – two hours later, three maybe. It made no difference. The weather had past, the fetid mist replaced by the now familiar sticky heat. Burn was asleep and snoring. I stood, careful not to wake him, and by the light of the same moon that shone on my Earth, I made my way off the mountain.

"Two days," my father said the next morning.

"A day and a half," I retorted.

"Two days," he repeated, "is enough time to settle in again. I thought you could assist me with the recording."

By recording, he was talking about the fucking bees again. To me, it was a waste of time. To my father, it was everything. I took the clipboard and flipped it in my hands. I hadn't seen Burn since I'd left him in the hollow. Was he okay? Was he safe? I wondered no more as his unmistakable form ambled through my peripheral vision. He didn't approach me and I didn't catch his eye.

My father and I trudged up the mountain. We chatted about the weather, the heat of the sun and his new best friend, Naylor. We didn't talk about the elephant in the room. It seemed neither of us had the courage to start the inevitable discussion.

"So, where's your mate?" my father asked as we drew level with the scary hollow that now appeared serene. Was he also a bloody telepath?

"What mate?" I was being pedantic.

"That guy, Burn. You haven't left his side for two days."

I glared at him. "I have and how should I know his movements?"

"Have you fallen out?"

"No, Father, we haven't fallen out because we never fell in." I pushed ahead. A deep chuckle from my father woke an angry beast inside me. I stopped, spun on my heels and threw the clipboard at him. It was a good aim; it smacked him right on the forehead. "Record the fucking bees yourself if you think it's so funny," I yelled.

Oh shit, I'd sworn at my father *and* hit him with a clipboard. Now I was in trouble.

"Edward!" His face turned purple and his eyes disappeared into two creases as he bared his teeth in pain or anger. I wasn't going to stick around to find out.

I ran.

In the village, I stopped and pressed my palms against my knees. As I was trying to steady my breathing, a shadow fell across my feet. Without looking up, I knew it was Burn – no one else came near the strange boy from another planet.

"I am guessing the work with your father did not go to plan."

"Your guess is correct, Sherlock." Standing up, I said, like a small child pleading for ice cream, "I want to go home."

"You have not given it enough time, Edward."

Fighting an urge to jut out my bottom lip, I muttered, "I don't want to. Will you take me or not?"

"No," was the simple reply.

"Fine. I'll take myself," I retorted and marched towards my crannog. Burn followed me in.

"You are a defeatist, Edward Kemp."

Burn had a fucking annoying habit of striking the wrong chord. Bringing my fist around in a wide arc, I swung for his face. With lightning reactions, he caught my wrist and jammed it down by his side. The momentum of the punch forced my body into his and we both propelled into the wooden wall of the house. It swayed ominously for a second. With Burn's hand still grasping my right wrist, I pushed my left arm across his chest and crushed my weight into him.

He brought his face level with mine. We were a thumb's width apart. For a long moment, we inhaled each other's air. Burn slowly ran his tongue along his lower lip before saying, "If you do not release me, I will wander my spare hand under your shirt and across your naked torso. Only the gods will know where it ends up."

Heat flushed through my body as I let him go with a raise of my arms and a loud string of expletives. Plonking myself on to the bed, I put my head in my hands. My skin was damp and my long fringe was wet. I was so tired of the heat on this planet. Burn sat next to me. "Fuck off," I spat and shifted away. He didn't. Sighing, I swung my legs up on to the bed and placed the pillow over my face.

A subdued silence followed. Burn was so quiet and still that if it wasn't for his weight pressing on the mattress, I'd have presumed he'd gone.

"I'm gonna have to speak to him, aren't I?" my muffled voice said.

"Yes."

"What do I say?"

"Tell him how you feel."

"Feel? My father doesn't talk about his feelings. Never has." Sitting bolt upright, I threw the pillow in the air; it landed in a pile of dust in the corner. "You can be my go-between. You can talk to him for me."

"No." Burn took my hand and pulled me off the bed. We stood facing each other. I'd never noticed that one of his eyes was paler than the other. "Come on." He shoved me out into the bright light of noon. I squinted at him – with his arms crossed and his legs planted apart, he was serious and it pained me to note that he was right. I had to talk to my father. The longer this went on the harder it was for either of us to break the ice. Burn and I made our way up the long mountain path.

"Burn, what happened in that hollow?"

"I told you to forget it, Edward."

"Something spooked you."

Burn knotted his fingers behind his back, lowered his head, and increased his stride. I guessed the conversation was over.

We came across my father, clipboard in hand, grovelling through a bush that resembled a lilac plant. They were my mother's favourites. He looked up, stared at us both for a moment, and then sat on his heels. He nodded once in my direction. "Edward."

"Father." I nodded back.

He threw down the clipboard and rubbed an angry bruise above his eyebrows. "Why do you insist on battling me at every turn?"

"Oh, good one, Father, start with a negative."

He stood and took a step forward. I took a step back and bumped into Burn, who shoved me forwards.

My father pointed at me. "I bought you everything you wanted and you've had an easy life."

"I didn't want things," I spat.

"Well, then, what did you want?"

"Your fucking time."

"Don't swear, Edward."

"Fuck. Fuck. Fuckerty fuck."

"Edward, don't be childish."

I put my face in my hands, screamed, and stamped my feet in the dirt. The tantrum only underlined my father's point.

My father straightened and edged forward. "Edward, my work is important."

"Oh yes, I'd forgotten that you're the mighty Herb Kemp." I stepped towards him. "You gave Abaytor and its people the love you should have given me."

My father shook his head. "You are too sensitive, boy."

"Is it sensitive to be hurt by your absence?" I made a fist and took a step forward. Burn placed a steadying hand on my shoulder that I shook off.

"There is no such thing as feeling hurt; you are just feeling sorry for yourself." My father grimaced as if he wished he hadn't said that.

"You bastard!" I swung for him but missed as Burn dragged me away. A look of shock – no, fear – crossed my father's face as he staggered backwards. I wriggled against Burn's grip but he held me firm. My chest ached and my nose had started to run. Taking a deep breath, I looked over my shoulder at Burn who gave me a slight nod and that small movement said he would stick by any decision I made. Turning back, I hissed, "You said you'd loan me the cataraft. I'm going to take it and go home."

My father gave a small nod and a half-hearted shrug. "Suit yourself. I tried."

"Tried! You're a long way from trying!" I shouted as tears welled and my shoulders quaked. Burn's hurried footsteps followed as I stomped away from him.

"You need to learn to control your temper, boy," my father called. "You get that from your grandfather."

I made to turn, to tell him I was nothing like my grandfather, to tell him if I had a son I wouldn't treat him in the way he treated me, but Burn drove me forward and away from the man who called himself my father.

An hour later, as we gathered supplies, I couldn't stop myself from snapping at Burn. "Can you just get on with it?"

"You are so impatient, Edward." Burn lifted the water vessel from the stream, tied off the neck and slung it over his shoulder. "You need to learn to – what is it you say – chill?"

"Don't tell me what to do." Battling through waist-high itchy grass, I stormed ahead of the boy. "Everything you do is so slow. You don't seem to know the meaning of haste." Nothing moved beyond a snail's pace on this stupid planet. "How long?"

"For what?"

"Until we get to the Landing Plains."

"The journey will be too long if you stay in this mood," Burn muttered and strode ahead.

We packed the cataraft within ten minutes. When I say pack, it was more like dump. In my temper, I'd chucked my belongings in willy-nilly. T-shirts, socks, boxers, and sandals mixed with Burn's bow, arrows, dagger, and torn shirt in a kind of weird art formation. I was sure I could've sold it for two million to the Tate Modern.

I pushed the raft away from the riverbank and into the copper flow of the river.

"Hello, Edward. Do you want me or not?" Burn's voice hollered from behind me.

In my rush to leave, I'd forgotten him. I rolled my neck, and heaved the craft back in. Burn jumped aboard and winked. "I knew you wanted me."

"I'm not in the mood for your games, Burn," I snarled.

"It seems not." He sat on a seat with a thump and swivelled away from me.

With the small motors at full tilt, the cataraft made good progress. Burn and I exchanged only a few words throughout the day. Once in this frame of mind, nobody can bring me round. Burn had clearly decided to abandon me to my mood.

With the setting of the sun, I grounded the cataraft on a small shale beach. An undulating countryside surrounded us. It reminded me of the rolling dales near where we lived. It amazed me how similar Abaytor was to Earth, as if they'd been ripped apart at birth and drifted away from each other. Groves of trees with small purple fruits, similar in appearance to plums, grew in poker-straight lines. I'd learnt, to my expense, to check before I ate anything from a tree. Thinking that an apple-shaped fruit was an actual apple, it had turned out to be what Burn called a Tummy Twirler, and I was sick for hours after one bite. Even though Burn now assured me that the fruits were good to eat, I had no appetite. Instead, I lay back and watched a ladybird crawling up my arm. Well, I hoped it was a ladybird and not some poisonous vampire beastie. On a distant hill, a forest stood ragged against the horizon, like torn black paper. A lake below it, with its evening silver sheen, mirrored the forest exactly. It reminded me of collages I had done at school. I shut my eyes and thought of happier days when Abaytor was just a dream in my father's overactive imagination.

The icy stones under my back took my breath. I had no idea of where I was, how I came to be there, or why there was a dark cloud hanging metres from my face. All that consumed me was the bitter cold. My numbed mind longed to sleep and never wake up. I forced my frozen hands to pat down my body. Was I hurt? My clothes were ragged and wet. I brought my hand to my face. Blood ran through my fingers and down my arm. I closed my eyes and mouthed one word repeatedly. Burn.

I don't know how much time passed before strong arms wrapped around my waist and muffled words came to my ears. With no strength to support my head, it dropped back as someone carried me away. I opened my eyes: my world was upside down and grey. The only clear shape I could make out was a tower with black slots for windows and a huge door. I shut my eyes.

"His situation is grave," a gruff voice said.

Thick liquid dripped on to my chest. Its contact with the skin caused a pulsing pain, like a toothache, only ten times worse. I arched my back off the bed and screamed.

Hands held my shoulders down. "Whether he will live until morning, I cannot say."

"Tell me what I can do?" The lilting tones of the young male voice were unmistakable. I opened my mouth to say his name but nothing came out.

"You cannot do anything, I am afraid. I am doing everything in my power. You may sit with him through the night."

"I will stay with him for as long as it takes." Burn took my hand in his.

I came to again, in pain with no idea of how long I'd slept. "Where the fuck am I?"

Burn had fallen asleep with his head on the bed, his hand still in mine. He awoke with a start and sat bolt upright. His face, creased from the sheets, slackened with surprise. "You are safe now. We are with the Ageless."

"Who? What the hell happened?"

"The Bad Thing."

"What was that? An animal?"

"No. It takes on many forms. It feeds off your fears and twists them into a reality. You are lucky to be alive."

I gently pulled my hand away. Burn's pale face flushed.

I awoke, sweating and panting.

"Edward?" Burn was kneeling by my side.

What the *hell?* My dreams were so vivid on Abaytor that I was positive Burn's telepathy was rubbing off. "Burn, what's The Bad Thing?" I whispered.

He looked away and said, "Why do you ask?"

"In my dream, you told me The Bad Thing caused my injuries."

Burn was quiet for a moment, as if he was scrabbling around for the words, then he looked back and said, "It is nothing. Just a dream," and gave me a thin smile.

I reached for his arm and pulled him back. "It's not *nothing*. It's why the mist in the hollow frightened you. Isn't it? And the warning from the Haruspex." My firm grip demanded answers.

He drew a breath and said, "It has many names. The Unseen. The Bird of Ill. The Penumbra. We call it The Bad Thing –"

"That's original," I interrupted.

Burn scowled at me before continuing. "It comes from nowhere and destroys all in its path."

"You told me that it has many forms." My stomach rolled over with the notion I'd had a premonition.

"Yes and no. It is a flash out of the corner of your eye. A sensation. A shiver. But it also takes on the shape of your fears and angsts."

"Nobody's seen it?"

"No. But there have been tales of mysterious disappearances."

"Lovely! This planet just gets better and better."

"But, on a positive note," Burn said cheerily, "it seems you have the gift of sight."

"Oh, God, I hope not. You don't know some of the dreams I've been having of late!"

"I have an idea." Burn raised an eyebrow and bit his lip.

"Of course you do." I sighed and elbowed past him. The shale crunched under my feet as I paced the beach. "So let me get this straight. The dream where I'm injured by The Bad Thing will come true?"

"Maybe."

The boy was infuriating. I planted my hands on to the inflatable sides of the raft and leaned in. "What do you mean *maybe*?" I growled.

"I believe that all human beings have the gift of sight. Some of us choose to use it and some choose to ignore it. I think Abaytor has brought your gift to the fore, whether you like it or not."

"Meaning?"

"Meaning, yes, it may come true."

Flinging my hands in the air, I spun on the spot. "Well, that's just peachy. Now what?"

"We cannot do anything but wait." He hesitated before murmuring, "Am I in your dream?"

I sighed and sat with a bouncy thump on the raft side. Burn would feed off my next words for some days to come. "Yes. You saved me."

Burn gave me a wicked smile. "Was I your knight in shining armour?"

It was odd to hear those words coming from Burn. I laughed, despite myself. "Yes, I suppose you were."

The stupid grin on Burn's face stayed there throughout the evening meal and all the way through to settling down.

That night, I discovered a fear of falling asleep. I didn't want to dream about Burn's hand down my trousers or of gaping wounds in my chest. I screwed my eyes shut and conjured up an image of my mother, sitting by the Christmas tree, smiling at me. Then, in the annoying way my brain works, Burn sauntered into the room and sat down next to her. I opened my eyes and blinked him away.

To my relief, in the few hours' sleep I got that night, I didn't dream. In fact, I didn't dream of anything in the nights it took us to reach the *Copper Queen*. She was still a ramshackle collection of wood and twine, but I'd never realised how glorious she looked. Burn was aboard with no discussion of whether we were going to continue on her or not. He peered at me expectantly. The cataraft was fast, light, and manoeuvrable but it was my father's. The *Queen* was slow, rickety, and unreliable but she represented freedom. There was no contest.

Pulling the cataraft alongside the *Queen*, I chucked equipment and belongings at Burn who flapped his hands in their general direction like a three year old. Everything ended up in a heap on the deck. "Your catching is rubbish. Did no one play ball with you when you were a kid?" As soon as the words were out, I wanted to swallow them. Burn did not have a childhood.

"No, Edward, no one played *ball* with me. What is that, anyway?"

"You know, you chuck a ball at one another."

"Sounds, um, stimulating."

"Was that sarcasm?"

He grinned at me. "It might have been."

I moored my father's craft, hopped on to the *Copper Queen,* and plonked myself on to one of the barrel seats. It was even good to feel the hard rim digging into my legs again. Burn pushed the raft off into the gentle flow of the copper water.

We meandered through flat exposed grasslands with the river tranquil underneath. Herds of beasts that looked like stretched brown cows looked up with startled expressions as we passed. They probably didn't get many visitors. And, next to the raft, water birds – I don't want to say ducks but they resembled them – floated along in our wake. Burn chucked scraps of his disgusting green weed bread to them.

"You know, bread is junk food to a duck."

"Junk and duck? What are those words?"

"Good name for a band, Junk and Duck." I stood and threw my arms out in a dramatic T-shaped pose. "Please welcome on stage – *The Junk and Ducks* with their new song, *The Green Weed Bread*."

"What are you talking about?"

"Nothing." I sat on a barrel with a thud and then changed my mind and lay out flat on the deck, stretching my limbs one by one until they popped. My eyes closed as my mind wandered.

Burn took my hand and led me through the shallows towards the waterfall. He was fully clothed. I was naked. I wrenched away from him.

"Relax, Edward."

If he tells me to relax one more time, I will deck him. "Is this entirely necessary?" *I growled.*

"It is worth a try." *Burn removed a folded piece of parchment from his bag and carefully peeled back the thin layers.*

"You know, Burn, I wouldn't be surprised if you made this whole thing up so you can see me naked – and wet."

"Edward! How can you say such a thing?" He flashed an eyebrow.

I swear, the last thing I would do before getting on my ship, was punch Burn. "Can we just get on with it?" *I chattered. I was losing the feeling in my legs as the glacial water rose and fell around my knees.*

Burn positioned me under the spray of the fall. I was grateful I wasn't expected to submerge fully in the icy water. His eyes flashed with mischief as he took two long strides back. He paused.

"Get. On. With. It," *I stuttered, as the cold water dripped off my hair and into my eyes.*

Oh, so now I dream. I rubbed my eyes and squinted into the daybreak.

Burn was by my side chopping leaves. He was a proper little Jamie Oliver. "So where are you taking me today?" I growled. I'd definitely woken up on the wrong side of the raft and was in no mood for one of his sightseeing trips.

"You will see."

I pushed stray hair out of my eyes. "You're supposed to be taking me to the Landing Plains."

"And I will. Be patient, Edward."

"I am being fucking patient."

He smiled at me in the annoying way he does.

Chapter Seven

A dry wind beat a surrounding grove of odd stunted trees as we forced our way through a thick patch of undergrowth and saw, on a steep-sided hill and at the mercy of the weather, a round tower. Stones the colour of rusty tin formed the base, and a wooden funnel arrangement topped it off. The only opening was a small round door painted green, like a Hobbit's dwelling. I craned my neck and squinted into the sunlight to view the top.

"What's it for?" I asked Burn who'd, without warning, invaded my space. Was this habit a conscious thought on his part?

"The Kooka people call it the Singing Tower. Its sole purpose is to broadcast their timeless chants. It forms part of their religious ceremonies. Today, they are offering thanks to the Ancients." Burn took my hand and pulled me towards the Tower.

"Ancients?" I yanked my arm away and brought a hand up to shield my eyes. The glare of Abaytor was insufferable. The light was brighter and the colours were stronger than on Earth and no one had told me to bring my Ray-Bans. My father had explained that the brilliance was down to the lack of pollution. I studied the far distance. There were other similar towers lined up on hilltops. I assumed the Kooka had positioned each tower to pass on the songs of the preceding – like primitive telephones.

Burn clasped my hand again and tugged me down on to the sweet-smelling grass. "Sit. Listen. This is a true honour."

I wrenched my hand away. *Good God, this kid was annoying.* I sat cross-legged to one side of a well-worn path that led to the tower. The grass was damp, and despite the warmth of the day, a chill crawled up my spine. I shuddered.

"Would you like a fur fetching?"

"I hope you're not reading my mind," I spat.

"I told you, I cannot turn it on like that. It comes when I do not expect it. I saw you shiver, that is all."

Damn it. Why was I so quick to jump down his throat? He was just being kind. "I'm okay. Thanks."

I heard them before I saw them. Low sounds that rolled through the woodland at the base of the hill and up into my waiting ears. The Kooka people were shorter than I'd imagined, and rounder. It was clear they were finding more to eat than I was. They walked two abreast, about twenty people, and there was a clear difference between the men and women. Proud like peacocks, the men wore jewelled robes of ultramarine and high headdresses of feathers. In stark contrast, the peahen women wore what looked like flour sacks tied in at the waist with string, no shoes, and carried burning incense sticks. At the head of the procession, and chanting the loudest, was a man with his face smeared in gunge and dressed from top to toe in red. He hauled a goat behind him.

"Burn, why do they have a goat?" I asked, but knew the answer.

"We call them capra. It is a sacrificial offering."

I watched in morbid fascination as the man tugged the capra up the path. It sprang to try to loosen the tight rope around its neck and called out a long pathetic bleat.

I turned away as the wretched ensemble passed and tried to remember I was on another planet in another age. The following procession passed in a haze of song and the smell of cinnamon wood. The chants were different, some low voiced with no discernible words, while some were high, and I could hear all the words. They all harmonised into one song.

"This is the good bit." Burn brought his long hands up in a prayer manner and rested them on his lips.

"When they kill the goat?" I'd been a vegetarian for a few years. It was the trendy thing to do at the time. I even joined an animal activist group. In the end, the downfall of most vegetarians was also mine – a bacon sandwich.

"It is an integral part. I have been told about this ceremony and have always wanted to witness it." Burn had never before travelled far from his home in the Fire Glade. Nobody in his tribe had. I recognised a desire in him: to break away from expectations. A sudden urge to take his hand, to connect to him, came over me. I fought it down.

The weird procession entered through the round door and disappeared. Burn stood and dragged me up with him. The chants of the Kooka people had escalated and the large wooden funnel magnified the sound. Then it stopped. Dead. All I could hear was the goat, Burn's quickened breaths and a loud, strangulated cry.

"The goat, I presume."

Burn opened his mouth to answer but shut it again with a pop as the Kooka sang the most haunting song I'd had ever heard. The hairs stood up on the back of my neck and my mouth slackened as the evocative tunes made me feel strange, relaxed, and happy.

The sun was making its way towards the horizon when Burn pulled at my hand. "It is time to move. I want to eat before sundown."

My belly rumbled its reply. "How did you know the Kooka ceremony was today?" I asked as we thrashed our way through the thick undergrowth back to the raft. The people of Abaytor had no clocks, telephones, or the internet. Burn's abilities amazed me; he told the time without a watch and knew where we were without a compass.

"There's been a good rainfall and at this time of the year the crops need the water. We were close to the Singing Tower and at the right time of the day. So the Kooka would be giving thanks to the Ancients." Burn stopped thrashing the bushes and stared at me. "Your people have lost the power of observation."

It troubled me to agree with him. All my friends seem to have their faces permanently stuck to some screen or another.

A cape of mist draped the river; it flapped up the banks and curled around our feet. The strangled cry of the unknown echoed and faded. Burn stiffened and I sensed his apprehension in the air.

"What?"

"Nothing."

"There's something."

"How do you know?"

"Um, dunno."

He laughed and hopped on to his *Queen*. She swayed as if to a soft song, against the banks of a sandy inlet. She looked peaceful in the dying light and dressed in a hazy petticoat. I almost harboured affection for her. I stepped aboard, centralised my footfall and she hardly moved. I rejoiced at my small victory.

A few of the wooden crates on her deck had remained tantalisingly unopened. Burn unsheathed his dagger. "Which one shall we open – the brown square one or the brown square one?" His eyes sparkled with mischief.

"I think the brown square one," I replied and smiled at him.

Burn's face lit like a flash of sunlight as he prised open the top of the crate and took a step back.

Then he was gone.

He'd dropped into the water and disappeared. There was no wild thrashing of arms or yelling, just a soft slap. There was no reason for him to go under – the river was calm and shallow near the shore. Time slowed as I ran across the deck, scanning left to right with mounting panic and cursing the misty brown water. I yelled his name repeatedly and falling to my knees, I swept my hands through the water, dividing the rolling mist in great waves. He can't have drowned, he's a strong swimmer, he was born on the river, I rationalised. Then, the unmistakeable shape of a copper allagarta swam into view.

Burn had told me tales about the beast. Like alligators, but three times the size and a brownish colour. He said their colouring aided their stealth in the copper water, and they'd developed a taste for human blood. One of Burn's stories was of an old man, who had gone to the water's edge to watch for his son returning from a fishing trip. The old man never found his son; instead, his son found a trail of blood leading into the water and a solitary slipshoe.

I feared for Burn – and for myself. This planet was a scarier place without him, and if he knew I thought that, he would laugh so hard.

Alone in the dark, with only the night cries and my over-active imagination for company, my heart pumped in my ears as I lit a torch and swung it out across the misty water. Nothing. Intending to search as far as my courage would allow, I leapt ashore and took a step downriver. An animal track weaved its way along the bank. Following it, I hoped it wasn't the track of a copper allagarta. Sweeping the torch to the left along the shore, I shouted Burn's name. Sounds in the still of the night bounced around eerily. Pushing on, my sketchy plan was to walk as far I dared, then, if I didn't find Burn, I would launch the raft at first light and explore the opposite bank. Something fluttered past my face; I jumped, and then froze. *Fucking* hell, this wasn't funny.

Building a rhythm to block out the creepy night noises, I stepped forward, swept the torch, and shouted Burn's name. I continued until a nagging fear nibbled at my brain and made me stop in my tracks.

Turning, my foot caught a root and I went down. The breath was forced out of my lungs and the torch flew from my grasp, rolled, and extinguished in the river.

I lay for a moment gathering my breath and my wits. How in God's name had I, Edward Kemp, son of the famous Herb, ended up in my own version of *Scary Movie*? This was as far as my courage allowed. I made my way back, half-blind, to the relative safety of the *Copper Queen*.

Under the star nursery sky, I forced down some dried meat and crawled under the furs. This was not how I imagined my time on Abaytor. I should be at home, drinking champagne and catching up with my mates, not alone on another planet perched on a piece of flotsam. What I wouldn't give for my home comforts right now. But those desires were useless. What I needed right now was Burn. I missed his shape next to me.

The water lapped at the raft with annoying repetition. Had my father given my perilous journey a second thought? Did he even consider that I might be in danger? I didn't believe that he did. If I died out here alone on the river, would he grieve? He didn't appear to grieve for my mother. On the January day we cremated her, his face was as frozen as the ground. Wrapping another blanket around my shivering body, I shut my eyes and hoped to sleep, if only for a short time.

Sunlight crept through a crack in the canvas and struck one eye. My body was awake in an instant, but I'm not sure my mind was. I groggily pushed the *Queen* into the water's flow. Ramming the pole into the riverbed, I hauled the raft over to the other bank. There, using a combination of pole and weight bearing, I managed to float her along straight enough, and combed the riverbank for any signs of Burn. This part of the river was featureless; shingle banks, a man's height, rose above the surface of the water. If he were here, I would have spotted him straight away.

Then, something caught my eye – a glint of light coming from a rocky inlet. I elbowed the raft on to the beach and jumped ashore sweeping eyes from river to bank. To one side of a clump of waterweeds, reflecting the sun, was a piece of jewellery. Intricate copper wire twisted around an aquamarine stone. Without doubt, it was Burn's pendant. It was a start. Blowing a long breath, I glanced around and flinched at the sight in front of me.

Twenty paces back from the water's edge were the remains of a forest. The trees lay haphazardly like dead soldiers on a battlefield. I scrabbled up the bank and took a tentative step towards it. The earth was sodden underfoot. Something terrible had happened here. The sky was violet and clear, but there was a stench of death and a smoky smell that I was sure would never leave me. Quickening my pace my feet sank into the saturated earth. With a sinking heart, I stared at my destroyed Mika 2020 sneakers. The sole was lifting off at the front and my socks were already sopping. I had bought them for strutting, not hiking. A cracking noise spurred me into a run. I vaulted a toppled tree and bellowed across the lifeless forest for Burn.

An answer came from the shadows. I halted and strained my ears. The words came from a tight coppice. "Edward. Here." Scrambling towards the sound, I found him, hollow-eyed and pinch-faced, slumped on his side in the mud.

"Burn!" I dropped to my knees and shook him hard with relief. He looked at me with a faraway stare. "Goddamn it, Burn, I thought you were dead."

"And who would have got you to your ship?" He flicked a smile and screwed up his face. "How did you find me?"

I placed the pendant into his open palm. "You dropped this."

Burn closed his fingers around it. "Thank you. It is the only thing I have left of my mother."

A surprising wash of relief swept over me. Was that because I'd found the guide to get me home or was it because I'd found Burn?

I tried to raise him but he let out a low moan and, for the first time,

I noticed his leg, bloody from knee to toe. The sight turned my stomach. "What happened?"

Burn struggled to reply. "I recall little. I do know a copper allagarta took me." He nodded towards his wound, "I kicked out in a desperate hope of connecting with any soft part. I had a lucky strike. The beast released its grip. I came to the surface far down river. I fought for the bank and crawled as far as I could. The allagarta do not travel more than a few body lengths from the water."

Slipping my arms around him my fingers felt every rib and the smooth concave of his stomach. I hauled him to his feet and slung his arm around my neck. He trembled under me. "Can you walk?"

"Enough to make it to the *Queen*." He took a tentative step and drew a raw breath.

I lugged him toward the riverbank. "I have a sense The Bad Thing has paid this place a visit."

"You are probably correct."

Burn's feet hardly touched the ground as I pulled him with renewed vigour. This conversation could continue another time; I had no desire to find out more about The Unseen or whatever it was called. We reached the water's edge and the *Copper Queen* had gone.

We stood for a long moment in silence. I replayed the last half hour in my head. The rock-strewn bank in front of us was, without question, where I'd left her.

"Edward, did you tie her up properly?" Burn asked, breaking the silence.

"I don't think I tied her up at all."

"Edward!"

Burn's shout made me lurch. "I had other things on my mind!" I yelled, and released my grip.

He fell to the ground with a thud, groaned and then muttered, "Edward, there is only one way she could have gone. If we follow the river we will, if the gods are with us, discover her in one piece."

Annoyed at my own stupidity and Burn's calmness, I hauled the boy back to his feet. We set off along the riverbank. I half-carried him in my eagerness to find the *Queen*. Our lives depended on a floating assortment of wood and I found that a ridiculous situation to be in. I didn't know how far we'd travelled – one *flow* maybe – when Burn pleaded for rest. Placing him on to a nearby rock, I stretched out my weary limbs. It was so quiet. I had found that, apart from nature's chatter, this planet was eerily silent. I was used to incessant noise – television and radio advertising to your subconscious. The noise of man-made machines and the background din of billions of people.

Burn's face was pale and his eyes were distant. We needed to find the *Queen* and fast. He rumbled a low moan as I dragged him back into my arms. I marched off at a fair pace but it wasn't long before my arms screamed for relief as Burn pressed his whole body weight into me. Finally, rounding a bend in the river's course, we saw the *Copper Queen* wedged into overhanging branches. "There she is." I could have wept.

Sitting Burn on the beach, I waded into the shallows, pulled her out of the trees, and tied her tightly to a stump. Then, using his leather bag as a pillow, I laid Burn on the deck.

"Edward, in the medicine crate you will find symphytum and achillea. I need you to grind these with a little water into a healing poultice."

I unfastened the crate that contained the medicines. It was a mass of green leaves and stems. How was I supposed to understand what anything was? "This one?" A stem of long grey-green grasses hung from my fingers.

"No."

"This one?" I gathered up some twisted black stems with shrivelled pods on the end.

"Yes, that is achillea. Look for a dark brown distorted root – that is the symphytum."

I found the root, took the achillea, and placed them in a small copper bowl. Using a rock, I ground the herbs with a little water into a pulp. Burn nodded and smiled at my creation.

As I ripped his breeches off from the knee down I flinched. There were three or four – it was hard to count under the amount of blood – deep lacerations.

Kneeling by his side, I forced a smile. "You'll be fine."

With Burn calling instructions, I managed to clean the wounds, apply the poultice, and bandage his leg. Rocking back on my heels, I nodded to myself. I, Edward Kemp, had performed a medical procedure on a raft on another planet. I didn't know I had it in me.

Burn slept much of the day and into the night. I picked up his fishing rod with the intention of catching supper before realising I had no idea how to fish. So I dozed, watched little blue birds flit across the water, and ate a little from our supplies before giving in to my own exhaustion.

The dawn brought a new and unknown day. Burn was sitting up and staring at me. "What?" I grumbled and heaved myself to my feet. "How are you feeling?" I inquired with a little more grace.

"Good. You did a great job with my leg, Edward. You would make a good Doctor of Medicine." He grinned and crawled over to release the raft from its moorings. "I think we'll make it to the Obelisk Tundra for breakfast."

An hour later, I laughed aloud. Standing stiff and proud on a flat sandy plain was a countless number of tall round-topped protrusions. Some were the colour of the red dirt, and some were paler, almost pink. My immediate mind-in-the-gutter thoughts were that they resembled a display of toys in a sex shop. I turned to tell Burn my hilarious comparison but thought better of it. He had no word for battery, so I was pretty sure he had no word for vibrator.

Chapter Eight

I settled back against a bent obelisk and studied my companion, who was on his knees boiling a pot of water over a small fire. "You look pale."

"Are you concerned for my welfare, Edward?" He winked.

"No. No. I don't want you dropping dead on me before we've reached my ship, that's all."

"How thoughtful."

I rattled my dish. "What is this grit?"

"That is your breakfast."

"Is there anything else?"

"No, Edward, there is not."

I put the dish down, pushed it away, and patted the protrusion at my back. "What are these for?"

Burn stood, held his injured leg slightly off the ground, and stroked a smaller phallus close to him. "Fertility symbols. If two people touch them at the same time they will have a long and, um, rampant relationship."

I leapt up and strode away a few paces. "You're joking, right?"

"No. It seems we will be forever – entwined."

"Fuck off."

Burn sighed. "I am joking, Edward."

"You're not funny." I sat cross-legged, careful not to touch an obelisk, just in case. "So do you think we'll ever see it?"

"What?"

"The Bad Thing."

"Yes."

"When?"

"I cannot say." Burn picked up a stick and fiddled with it.

"You know, don't you?"

"Are you reading my mind, Edward?"

"I'm not a bloody telepath."

He chucked the stick and scooped handfuls of dust on to the fire. "Let us go. I am aware that I am slowing you down."

"Yes, you are." I pushed up and sauntered back to the raft. Burn followed with uneven footsteps. A shiver up my backbone made me spin round to find him leaning against an obelisk, clutching his stomach.

I remained where I was. "Are you okay?"

"Breakfast has disagreed with me."

"I'm not surprised."

Burn dropped to his knees and moaned. I hurried to his side and lifted him off the ground. "Is it the after effects of the allagarta attack?"

"I do not know," he breathed.

I hauled him to the raft and, for the second time in two days, laid him on the deck.

"What do you need?"

"Rest." His face was grey and black underlined his eyes.

I picked up the push pole. "Don't worry, I'm in control."

Burn groaned. "Now I am worried. Be gentle with her."

"Burn, it's a collection of wood."

"It is my collection of wood," he said before closing his eyes.

The river flowed fast past the Tundra, and the *Queen* made good progress. By lunchtime, Burn had improved enough to mosey around the raft tidying, and sighing. "Edward, are you this messy at home?" He held, between his fingertips and at arm's length, a used pair of undies.

I rammed the pole into the water. "I don't tidy at home."

"Why?"

"I have a, um, housekeeper."

"A servant?"

"No, she's not a servant, she is a, um."

"She cleans?"

"Yes."

"Cooks?"

"Yes."

"She is a servant."

"When you put it like that it sounds so – medieval."

Burn threw the offending underwear into the shelter.

"Hey! They were my last pair!"

"Oh, now you will have to be naked under your shorts."

"You're so fucking annoying and, it seems, depraved."

That evening, we tied up on the shore of a large derelict temple. On the side I could see, one of the two grey-stoned towers had collapsed and the right side of the building was covered in a luminous green plant that snaked into cracks and through broken windows. The walls had raw edges where the roof once sat, and the far left hand side was just a heap of rubble as if a giant had stamped on it. Amongst the ruins, jewels of colour glinted in the late light from the remains of stained-glass windows. A breeze stirred the trees that surrounded the church and the leaves whispered *stay away*, or my imagination thought they did.

Burn said, "I wish to explore the ruins in the morning."

"Fill your boots but I'm leaving at first light, with or without you." I plonked on to a honey barrel, tapped my foot on the deck, and fiddled with my watch, which was a gift from my mother and even though it stopped working weeks ago I couldn't bear to be parted from it. I felt like I'd left the iron on, or forgotten to lock the door. There was something in the air, or in the ruins. "Burn?"

"Yes."

"What was this place?"

"An ancient house of the gods."

"It gives me the collywobbles."

"Your colly is wobbling, how delightful."

"No, you idiot, it –"

"Edward …"

"What?"

"We need to run and we need to run now!"

"Why?"

Burn yanked me up by the scruff, shoved me on to the bank, and with a hand between my shoulder blades, propelled me forward.

"What the fuck, Burn?"

As I ran, brambles scratched at my exposed skin, and the uneven ground twisted my ankles. Burn, even with a battered leg, raced past me. He was a good ten paces in front of me when he glanced over his shoulder. With fear etched into his face he yelled, "Run, Edward. Run!"

"I *am* fucking running!" I yelled, and increased my stride. My lungs cried for relief and my arms ached as I pumped them to propel me forward. I caught up with Burn. He snatched my wrist and yanked me into a narrow mossy breach in a stone wall. We pressed, chest to chest, into the shadows as a smell of mould gusted up my nostrils. I could feel Burn's heart through my shirt; it matched mine for rhythm and pace. My head throbbed and my vision swam. I felt like I was in a *Marvel* film – a normal person isn't hunted through a ruined temple by a monster. Burn was staring past me and I knew at what. It compelled me to look. I couldn't resist. And there it was – an angry mass of black fog hovering a man's height above the ground.

"What the fuck?" I whimpered and froze. The *Thing* blocked the only escape route from the breach. My knees buckled. Burn grabbed me and yanked me up. Our tormentor twirled around before it sucked in the remaining evening light and became dark and solid. Its edges became sharper as it twisted and warped. Before my eyes, a humanoid shape formed. It hung motionless for a moment. I thought about my mother in better times; she was baking cakes with her flowery apron on. She stopped baking cakes when my father discovered Abaytor. Why was I thinking about my mother and her cakes? What the *fuck* was happening? I wanted to flee so badly, but the wall had become a trap. We had nowhere to go. We were at its mercy. Then, a smoky arm reached for me. Burn held me tight as I buried my head into his neck. A strong grip jerked me away from him. My arms flung backwards as my feet lifted off the ground. A biting cold nipped at my bones and the world went black.

The stones under my back were like ice. My whole body was shivering and I couldn't breathe. I longed to sleep and never wake up. Forcing my eyes open, I blinked furiously. Where was I?

Hanging above me was The Bad Thing. Its form was half-humanoid and half-trailing black mist. The murky head was pointing in my direction as if it were studying me. I tried to scramble away and opened my mouth to scream, but my frozen body wouldn't heed the commands from my brain.

My chest was wet and hurt like holy hell. I brought my hand to my face and blood ran through my fingers and down my arm. "Burn," I whimpered and passed out.

There was a lifting sensation. Was it The Bad Thing again? I didn't know, or care. If I had a will to fight, it certainly didn't show itself now. Strong arms wrapped around my waist, my head dropped back as friend, or foe, carried me away. I opened my eyes just enough to see the world was upside down and grey with the only clear shape a ruined tower with slot windows and a huge door. I shut my eyes.

"His situation is grave," a gruff voice said. Father? I opened my mouth to speak his name but only dry air formed.

Thick liquid dripped on to my chest. Its contact with my skin caused pain like a toothache, but a hundred times worse. I arched my back and screamed.

Hands held my shoulders down. "Whether he will live until morning, I cannot say."

"Tell me, what can I do?"

The lilting tones of the young male voice were unmistakable.

"You cannot do anything. I am doing everything in my power."

Burn took my hand. "I will sit with him through the night."

I passed out and came to again, in pain, with no idea of how long I'd slept. "Where … am … I?" I croaked.

Burn had fallen asleep with his head on the bed, his hand still in mine. He awoke with a jump and sat bolt upright. Dark rings circled his dull eyes, and he was paler than I'd ever seen him.

"We are with the Ageless."

"The Ageless?" I sighed and tried to crack the cricks in my neck.

"You have dreamt this?" Burn asked.

I stared at him. "You know I have. In the dream you told me The Bad Thing caused my injuries." I pulled my hand away from Burn's grasp. He blushed. Shuffling up on to my elbows, I looked around the room. I seemed to be in Snape's chamber from *Harry Potter*. The circular room had irregular plaster walls. Dust motes played in shafts of light coming from holes in the low wooden ceiling. One large timber door stood in front of me, and to either side of that were tall stained glass windows. At one time, the broken pictures were of a long-tailed comet in a purple starry sky. A bed, a table, a cupboard, and one chair were the only furniture. Dotted on every free surface were hundreds of candles and thousands of filled glass jars. Dried roots hung in rows from nails driven into the walls, and next to them, furry things that resembled rabbit's ears.

"What did The Bad Thing want with me?"

Burn shrugged. "I do not know."

The door creaked on its hinges as someone pushed it from the other side. An old man shuffled into the room. He had a hunched back, leaned on a tall stick with a blue glass ball on the top, and plaited his waist-length grey hair with purple ribbon to match his floor-scraping robe. He looked like a wizard from my childhood stories; he just needed a pointy hat.

Burn stood and bowed. Why was he bowing?

"Treater," he said.

Treater nodded and replied, "Burn." The gruff voice belonged to him, not my father. "How is the boy this morning?" he asked without looking at me.

"Because of you, he is a lot better."

"Hello. I'm here." I raised my hand and waved. Burn smiled at me.

"Edward, this is Treater. He saved your life last night."

The old man sat on the edge of the bed. "I'm grateful to you," I said before turning to Burn. "Though I'm sure I also have you to thank. How did you save me from The Bad Thing?"

"By the time I got to the courtyard where you were lying, you were alone. It was gone."

"Gone?"

"Yes. I do not know why it did not finish you off."

"It tried, though." I winced and placed a hand on my chest.

"Lie back. Your chest needs caring for," the old man said.

I did as he asked. There was something comforting about him – familiar, even. Treater disappeared into the shadowy depths of the room. Burn sat next to me and undid my top button, and then the next. I gripped his hand. "What are you doing?"

"Easy, Edward. I have to remove your shirt to change the bandages."

I let go. Burn proceeded, button by button, in an infuriatingly unhurried pace. He undid the last one and slid the shirt open. He sat me up, slipped the fabric off my shoulders, and then persuaded me to lie down again. Treater appeared with a bowl of foul-smelling grease in his hand.

"Is your name Treater? Or is that your profession?" I watched him undo my bandages.

"Both," he replied.

The wound on my chest was larger than I'd imagined and a perfect circle about the size of a saucer.

"Here," Treater handed Burn the bowl, "I have to fetch some water, but you can apply the poultice."

Burn took the bowl and eyed me for a long moment.

"You look tired," I said.

"Yes. I am not feeling myself." Burn dug his fingers into the bowl. "This will be cold, Edward." He slopped a large splodge of the grease on to my chest.

I hissed. Was everything in these damned ruins freezing? Burn worked the poultice slowly across my chest. I juddered under his cold fingers, but the sensation felt good. He moved in a gentle circular motion for a minute before sliding his hand away, stroking a long line down my rib cage, and encircling my navel. Why was I letting him do that? Burn glanced at me and bit his lip. I said nothing.

I sensed someone was observing us and peered over Burn's shoulder. Standing in the shadows, unblinking and unmoving, was Treater. Burn withdrew his hand. "You are done," he whispered and strode away. Treater silently reapplied my bandages and left the chamber.

The next day or two passed. I watched the light change through the stained glass and observed Burn. He was in his element, caring for me and having in-depth discussions with Treater about medicine. It appeared he had a vast knowledge of the plants and herbs needed, and some idea of how to prepare them. For those few days, Burn was a student doctor. It was no wonder he craved an escape from the Fire Glade; he had so much more to offer.

Treater seemed to be the only person living in the ruins. Where was the rest of the Ageless? I queried Burn one morning. He said that the people revered Treater, even worshipped him. So he was left to his own devices amongst the rubble of an ancient house of the gods. The people visited when they required healing.

On the third day, Burn hauled me out of bed. "That is enough lying around, Edward. You need some air; I thought I could teach you how to hunt."

On an earth bank near the ruins, I untangled my fingers from a bowstring and grumbled that I didn't need hunting skills in the wilds of suburbia.

"You are holding it wrong." Burn dropped his weapon and it bounced in the dirt, reflecting his impatience.

"Look, Burn, a bow and arrow are not a fashion accessory where I live." I swung the dragon-wood bow by my hips and resisted the urge to poke him in the side with the pointy end.

"Do you want to learn to hunt?"

"No. Maybe." I turned the weapon over in my hands. Burn had made it that morning. It had taken him the same amount of time as it had taken Treater to boil a pot of water.

"Here." He positioned himself behind me and slid his hands along my arms. Moving the bow back into place, he placed the arrow on to the rest, threaded the fingers of his right hand with mine, and drew back the bowstring. He blew softly on my neck as he controlled his breathing. "At the point of release," he whispered, "hold your breath." His fingers tightened, digging the taut string painfully into my skin. "Ready?" he breathed.

"Um." I hummed and held my breath.

Burn released my fingers which automatically released the arrow; it flew straight and pierced the centre of an upturned wooden crate he'd placed on the remains of a wall.

Nobody moved.

The bow remained at arm's length and Burn lingered behind me with his hands on my arms. "It hit," I said eventually.

"Now, you try." Burn moved to pick up his own bow.

I strode the ten or so steps to retrieve my arrow then returned to him.

Positioning my feet carefully I brought the bow up to eye level. I could feel Burn watching my every move and I was desperate to hit the crate; I needed to show him I wasn't entirely useless. Drawing my hand back until the arrow quivered on the string, I held my breath.

"Focus," Burn whispered.

Closing my eyes, I conjured up an image of the crate with my white-feathered arrow imbedded in it. I released the string and flicked open my eyes to watch the arrow's wide arc towards its target. It hit the wall, not the crate, but at least it hit something.

"Yay!" Burn bellowed and clapped me on the back.

I smiled at his enthusiasm.

"You will be catching our supper in no time."

His faith in me never wavered and a part of me fed off that.

On the fourth day, Burn said, "Treater needs some zingiber roots from the cellar."

I followed him towards a ruined stone archway. Through it and under a vaulted roof, the long steep flight of steps I'd seen in my dream led down into darkness. As I stood at the top, the smell of damp mixed with lavender was already strong. I peered at the shadowy ironbound door at the bottom. The sun was hot on my back and my chest hurt like hell. The cool of the cellar was inviting.

"Come, Edward." Burn grasped my wrist and pulled me behind him. I didn't pull away and assured myself I was in control: the dream didn't have to come true.

The arch of sunlight behind me grew smaller, and the air became cooler the further down we went. Someone had left the door unlocked and Burn heaved it open using his shoulder and a fair bit of grunting. I shoved it closed behind us, took a sharp intake of breath, and shivered. It was as I'd dreamed. The flickering light from the lone torch on the wall showed the racks of spears and the shelves of jars.

"You have seen this place before?" Burn asked.

"You know I have, Burn."

"This way." Burn led me past the helmets placed above breastplates – the waiting knights from my dream.

"Remind me again, why are we down here?" I pulled against the eagerness of his lead.

He stopped and moved in close. With his breath hot on my cheek, he said, "To find the zingiber root that Treater needs for your medicine."

My muscles tensed. He smelled like clean washing and his hair, which had tumbled over his eyes, shone bronze in the torchlight.

"Oh, yes," I croaked and scooted around him.

A hand caught my arm and held it firm. A charge was so thick in the air it could be tasted. My heart banged a beat as my body froze. Without turning, I murmured, "Burn, I don't *do* guys." I wrenched from his grip.

Burn slid around me and we stood face to face. He was always pale but in this light, he was radiant. He looked me in the eye. "You also do not *do* river rafting or sleeping under the stars or battling The Bad Thing or psychic dreaming. It seems, Edward Kemp, that you *do* more than you know." He leaned in.

I swear I wanted to run, but my legs wouldn't listen to the yelled orders from my brain. My mouth went dry. No. No. No. I could control this. I darted around him, paused, ran towards the door, wrestled it open, ran into the brilliant light of day, and sat heavily on a fallen column.

"I suspect this is not how your dream ended," Burn said from behind me.

I sighed and stared at the ground. "Nope. It ended with your hand down my trousers."

"How lovely!" The giggle in Burn's reply was infectious and maddening. I liked the boy and loathed him in unequal amounts. "Come with me, Edward. I promise I will not put my hand down your trousers." Burn took the first few steps down into the cellar and proffered his hand.

"You don't need me to get the root. I'll wait for you here." The cellar actually would have been preferable. There was little shade amongst the ruins and the midday sun was burning the back of my neck.

"You do not trust me?"

I didn't trust anybody. In my experience, everybody wanted something from me, be it fame by association or money. "No," I said bluntly. Burn's bright face dropped. I sighed and got up. After everything he'd done for me he deserved my trust.

Of course, the root was in the farthest corner of the cellar, down a corridor the width of my shoulders. "Why on Earth –" I corrected myself. "Why on Abaytor, do they keep it in such an inaccessible place?"

"I do not know. There must be a reason." Burn's narrow frame walked the corridor with ease. I scraped my elbows on its walls.

Hung from a nail was a large canvas sack. Burn unhooked the bag and dropped it to the floor. He opened it and inside were hundreds of shrivelled roots, ranging in colour from sickly yellow to black. He rummaged around and brought out a handful of dark green ones.

"Are you sure they're right?"

He hesitated. "Yes, I think so."

"Great. Let's go." I pressed my back against the damp wall as Burn hooked the sack back on its nail. It was cold and dimly lit in the narrow space, but I was hot. A gentle breeze from one of the many gaps in the ceiling wafted my fringe into my eyes. I pushed it aside. Burn squeezed into the tiny space in front of me and stopped. His eyes stared into mine and glazed over. Bloody telepath. I'm sure I felt him rummaging around. "Burn, stop it!" I squeezed my eyes shut and tried to close the doors in my mind.

"I have," he said. With care to avoid my wound, he placed an open palm on my chest and spread out his fingers one by one. The touch was light but potent. Seconds passed. Heat flushed my face and my stomach fluttered before I grabbed his wrist and yanked his hand away. We stood, squashed and motionless, breathing each other's air for a long moment. Fuck. Fuck. *Fuck.* I'd been pursued, wounded, and terrified within an inch of my life. In desperate need of attention, any attention, I released his hand and waited.

Burn squirmed away. "I made you a promise, Edward."

"Yes, yes. Of course. That's right." I caught myself mimicking my father's body language as I stood straighter and threw back my shoulders.

Burn avoided eye contact as we walked back to the Treater's chambers.

Chapter Nine

"Why are we on the cataraft again?" Naylor asked.

"You know why, old friend." Herb trailed his fingers in the warm copper water. The river moseyed through a vast plain and the light cataraft, without any power, seemed to hover above the surface, not getting anywhere fast.

"You are having a holiday." The tribal elder whittled away at a piece of wood.

"Correct."

"We may bump into the boys."

"They'll be long gone by now."

"You are hoping they are not."

"Get out of my head." Naylor was right; Herb did hope they'd run into the boys, he really needed to say goodbye to Edward on a better note. He didn't want their last words to be venomous. What he did want was for Edward to know that he was important, and would always be more important than Abaytor and even Herb's mission. But Herb knew he'd open his mouth to tell him just that, then shut it again. Above all, he really wished he could say 'I love you', but he also knew he was incapable of those three words. So, if he could say, 'See you later', and encourage Edward to continue with his studies when he got home, then that would have to do.

"I am sorry, it is just that you have such an interesting, um, head. There is so much knowledge and – activity," Naylor said.

Herb sat up straight and then shuffled over to sit by his friend's side. "I've been thinking and I have a theory about your Ancients."

Naylor looked up from his work. "Please tell."

"Okay. The wandering storytellers tell tales of the Ancients. They say, as you do, that they are the all-powerful gods."

"Yes."

"They tell a story that if the Ancients die, then all life on Heras dies."

"That is true."

"Well, I believe those all-powerful gods to be real."

"They are real."

"No, what I mean is tangible in some form or another."

"Explain."

Herb spoke slowly; he didn't want to get a single word wrong. "A few years ago, before I found your village, I stumbled upon a vast network of underground tunnels with wet walls, a terrible smell of rot, and a strange blue glow. They were too precise to be dug by animals, so I assumed that a tribe, or many tribes, lived in them. I have since learnt that no Abaytorians live underground." He took a breath. "They may be the haunt of your Ancients, Naylor. People who have lived underground for so long that time has forgotten them."

Naylor chewed his lip and stared at Herb for a long moment before saying, "You believe another race of people live on Heras?"

"More like under than on."

Naylor shook his head. "No, I would have heard about them."

"You *have* heard of them through the stories of the troubadours and legends passed down through families." Naylor still looked doubtful so he continued, "On Earth, there was a myth surrounding a giant squid called a Kraken. According to terrified sailors, the creature attacked and consumed whole ships. It was assumed that the tall-tales were the result of sea-weary men, until specimens were washed up on to beaches proving the myth was actually truth. So, there's no reason why your Ancients aren't real."

Naylor turned the wood in his fingers for a few moments before saying, "In recent years, I have sensed a disruption in the telepathic field that always coincides with your visits."

"Maybe the Ancients don't like me?"

"Or maybe they do …"

"Well." Herb smiled and shrugged. "What's not to like?"

"Shall I ask your son that question?"

"I think Edward would give you a long list of negatives." He picked at his fingers. It hurt that his son didn't like him, never mind love him. "So, what are you implying?"

"I am not sure. But if you are right, we will find out at the Basin."

"Basin?"

"It is said when you enter the bowl, you can feel the planet spin and time slows to a crawl."

The cataraft dropped suddenly and then reared at the front. Herb rolled across the deck and slammed into a wooden crate. Scrabbling on to his knees, he peered over the inflatable sides at a mass of broiling black fog. It bobbed a raft's length away from his face as if considering its next move. "What the hell is that?" he whispered with his throat dry and his heart missing every other beat.

"The Bad Thing."

"That's just a story made up to frighten children." Fog didn't have intelligence and didn't threaten humans, his scientist brain rationalised.

"Like the Ancients are just a story?" Naylor picked up the push pole and straddled Herb's crouching form.

Herb couldn't have a man twenty years his senior protect him from a make believe monster with a stick. That would not make a good story down the spaceship builders' yard. If anyone was going to defend Herb, it would be himself. He wriggled out from between Naylor's legs and stood. The Bad Thing shifted and turned but didn't advance.

"What are you waiting for?" Herb yelled. He wanted it to do something, either attack or leave; the silent hovering was pushing his blood pressure through the roof, and he'd forgotten his medication on this trip. The Bad Thing moved, but not towards him, away from him, then dispersed in the warm air like cigarette smoke.

Naylor put down the pole. "It was not your day."

"What the does that mean?"

"It was not your day to die."

"Die?"

"Yes, The Bad Thing is a killer."

Edward's face came to mind. "My son," he blurted. "Is he safe?"

Naylor closed his eyes and wrinkled his weathered forehead. "For now."

Chapter Ten

The *Queen* groaned under the weight of stuff Treater had donated. Fresh vegetables, bags of grain, bundles of herbs, and two coarse blankets littered her deck. I was sad to leave the old man and his ruins. I'd enjoyed his company and there was something reassuring about him. Unlike the sulky send-off I'd given my father, I waved with enthusiasm in his direction as Burn pushed off from the bank.

"Oh, did I tell you to beware of the Basin?" Treater shouted after us.

"No," I yelled back as we drifted further away.

Treater opened and closed his mouth in speech but by then we were too far away to hear his words.

"Beware of the Basin? What the fuck does that mean? Why does everybody talk in fucking riddles around here?"

Burn smiled and teased, "Even so, Edward Kemp, I do believe you like Treater."

I sat on a barrel and crossed my arms. "I do. He's not as annoying as you."

Burn swept the pole through the copper water as an early morning mist swirled around the raft. I shivered and rubbed my hands together. "It's just mist, right?"

"It is just mist, Edward. Do not worry, I will protect you."

"I'm sure you will."

"You do not give me the credit I deserve. I am stronger than I look and was saying to Treater just —"

Something to one side of the *Queen* caught my eye. I put my hand up to quieten him. A ball of mist had churned and darkened. The hair rose on the nape of my neck as I croaked, "Burn." The pole clattered as he dropped it. He appeared by my side. I jumped and then fought to stay upright. Run. Run. *Run.* My body wouldn't respond to the desperate cries from my brain. The Bad Thing rose from the surface of the water and grew to the size of the raft within two blinks of the eye. Long arms snaked from the dense mass and reached for me. I spun around, searching for something to hit it with, an escape route, I didn't know. There was nowhere to go; the raft was moving quickly in the middle of the wide river.

Burn shoved me hard and I teetered, spinning my arms and throwing one leg out for balance. "What the fuck, Burn?" I yelled before I toppled into the copper water.

The fast flowing current pulled me under and time passed while I whirled in confusion. Finally, a voice in my head said, *You're gonna die if you don't do something*. I pushed down on my legs in a frog-like movement and clawed my way out of the murky water and towards the light. I surfaced, flapping and gasping for air.

"Swim, Edward," Burn bellowed from the *Queen*.

But it was too late. The Bad Thing surrounded me like a swarm of mosquitos, lifted me out of the water and into Hell.

The only clue I had that I was alive was my heart hammering in my chest. I was screaming but I couldn't hear the sound. Spinning, limbs dangling free, in complete darkness, an all-consuming sorrow and utter despair swamped me. My mother dying on the pavement played repeatedly in my mind. And a longing to be with my father manifested itself into a physical pain in my chest.

A putrid smell filled my nostrils as an unbearable heat scorched my side. I screamed – well, I thought I did. The Bad Thing reacted by closing in and squeezing my body, forcing the air from my lungs. Long cold wisps probed under my clothing. Twisting my shoulders, I kicked out my legs, but the beast held me fast.

A deluge of water filled the silent void and I choked with every wave that engulfed my face. I tried to turn my head to get some air, but I couldn't move. Here was where it ended; this was where I died, drowned in a monster's belly on another planet. That, I didn't see coming; I always presumed it would be a heart attack while in bed with the local hottie.

Then The Bad Thing released me as quickly as it had taken me. There was a sensation of freedom before I smacked the river and went under for the second time. The monster had sucked any reason to live out of me, so I let the cold water consume me and I sank.

I awoke and blinked furiously into the light as a blurry face whirled into view. With a knee planted at either side of my waist, Burn straddled me and his weight pushed my hips into the rough gravel of the shore. He'd gathered my T-shirt up and firmly planted his open palms on my bare chest.

"What the *fuck* are you doing?"

"Saving your life."

"How, exactly?"

"Chest compressions."

With all the strength I could muster I yelled, "Get off!"

Burn hesitated, then duly slid off and lay on his side next to me.

"Where is it?"

"Gone."

"Where?"

"I do not know. But I do know it enjoys fire, but does not like water."

"So it was you that half burnt me and then topped it off by drowning me? Oh, and did I mention you pushed me in the river in the first place?!"

"Er, yes, but you are alive."

I eyed my singed trousers. "Er, scorched."

"Alive," Burn repeated.

I sighed. "Why does it only attack me?"

There was a guilty air about him as he said, "I think you may offer a better feast."

I propped up on to my elbows. The *Queen* looked woeful – tipped on to her side, with an overhanging branch holding her fast. The barrel seats bobbed in the shallows and my rucksack lay sopping on the shore. "Oh no, my stuff," I wailed. I didn't care what Burn had been through to end up with the raft in this position.

"They are just things, Edward. You have your life. Look on the bright side, now we know how to fight it."

I had despised it when my mother told me there was more to life than material items and I couldn't take them 'with me'. Now I would give up everything to have her back, if only for a moment. Despite the distance between us, I missed her.

"I guess you pulled me out. Thank you." However annoying Burn was, he had just saved my life. Again.

"You are welcome, Edward." Burn stood, squeezed the water from his sopping shirt, and then reached out a long hand. I took it and he heaved me to my feet. We stood staring at each other before he said, with a glint in his eye, "I have an idea." He yanked me towards the raft. "Take your clothes off."

"I shan't."

"Edward, it will not work if I am impeded by the fabric."

"You're making that up."

"I am not. Do you want me to do it for you?"

"No!"

Burn dropped with a thump on to a boulder and kicked a pebble into the water. The waterfall behind him sprayed a fine mist that blocked out the sky and the noise was deafening. "Edward. You will never make it to the Landing Plains alive unless you take your clothes off."

"Why me?" I whined and shucked off my shirt.

"I think The Bad Thing feeds off your fears and anxieties. It becomes a manifestation of them. The banquet your issues provide is irresistible."

"Lovely."

"Relax, all will be well." Burn made a little come-hither gesture. "And your trousers."

"You're enjoying this."

"A little maybe." He chuckled and then straightened up. "Trousers," he repeated.

This was turning into a bloody private striptease. I placed my hands on my hips. "Tell me again why I need to undress?"

"The fall cannot cleanse you fully clothed." He paused. "Do you want The Bad Thing to hunt you for the rest of the trip?"

"No. You know I don't."

"Then – trousers."

I undid the button, paused; unzipped the fly, dropped them, and stepped free.

"And the rest."

"Burn, I –"

"Edward, I have seen it all before."

"I don't wish to know your sordid past. And you've not seen mine before."

"Do you have a deformity?"

"What? No!"

"Then why are you worried?"

Twenty men sharing a rugby changing room shower and I don't bat an eyelid. But one skinny native on another planet and I come over all shy. I sighed and slid down my pants.

"Good." Burn slapped his knees. "It is time." He took a few paces towards me and stood in my space. His hair had tumbled into his eyes and he smelt like mown grass. His warmth radiated on my chest. Neither of us spoke or attempted to move. I was sorely aware of my nakedness, sorely aware I was out of my depth, and sorely aware that this boy had me eating out of the palm of his hand.

"Come on," he said softly and linked my arm. I pulled away and followed him through the shallows. Burn was fully clothed with a bow slung on his back and a pouch around his waist. I was naked. It was all far too weird.

The glacial water reminded me of my childhood marbles: copper in the middle and grey at the edges with a clear surface. As the fall cascaded over hidden rocks, a clear humanoid shape appeared and an over-long arm pointed straight at me.

"Burn, did you see that?"

Burn followed the direction of my stare. "What?"

"There's a person in the waterfall."

"I can't see anyone."

I looked at him then back at the fall. As if it'd been swept away with the water, the figure had vanished. "It's gone."

"What was it doing?"

"Pointing at me."

"Maybe it fancied you?"

"Burn!"

"Come on," he said without looking at me.

"Are you sure this is necessary?"

"It is worth a try."

"You know, Burn, I wouldn't be surprised if you made this whole thing up so you can see me naked – and wet."

"Edward! How can you say such a thing?" He shot me an injured look.

I didn't believe he was hurt for one second. "Can we just get on with it?" My teeth chattered and I was losing feeling in my legs as the freezing water rose and fell around my knees.

Burn positioned me under the fine spray of the waterfall. My feet stood on smooth, tumbled stones, which fitted together like crazy paving, and the cold water soaked my hair, which then dripped into my eyes. I was grateful he didn't expect me to submerge fully in the icy flow. Burn took two long strides back, stopped and smiled.

I cupped my lower regions. "Fucking. Get. On. With. It."

He removed a folded piece of parchment from his trouser pocket and carefully peeled back the thin layers.

"What's that?"

"Treater gave me it; he knew there was a connection between The Bad Thing and water. This is an ancient cleansing prayer." He flapped the paper in my face.

I stepped out of the icy spray. "It's a spell, isn't it?"

"Call it what you like. Please step back." Burn scanned the parchment, shut his eyes for a moment, then refolded it and put it back in his pocket. He took a small candle and flint from his leather bag and took several attempts to light the wick in the damp air. At that moment, I'd never wanted to punch anyone more than him.

"Be patient, Edward."

"I said nothing."

"You did not need to."

Of course I didn't. I stepped back, stamped my feet, and jiggled my shoulders. "Burn, I will have a bloody heart attack if I stand in this fucking water for another second!"

Burn held the candle close to his body and formed a roof above it with an open hand. He shut his eyes and dropped his head.

He chanted, *"Power of the elements five, help this boy to stay alive. From red Earth to moving air, past burning fire that magic flare. Flow with water, lake, and fall, help this boy to conquer all."*

The words were quiet at first, almost drowned out by the roar of the waterfall. On the second speaking, he was louder, and on the third, Burn threw his hands up and bellowed towards the sky. He stayed in the Y-shaped position for a minute or two. If I could have felt my foot, I would have tapped it.

Finally, he waded towards me and scoured the water at our feet. "Where is my candle?"

"It flew off during your dramatic moment."

He stuck out his bottom lip before saying, "Do you feel any different?"

"Nope."

"It may take time."

"Are we finished? My bones are frozen."

"Yes. Do you want me to warm you up?"

"NO!" I pushed past him and as fast as my numb legs allowed, marched out of the lake and threw on my trousers and shirt.

That night, as I listened to his soft slumbering breaths, he occupied my thoughts. I'd given him so much grief on this journey, including battling The Bad Thing. Yet, with nothing but the clothes on his back and the spread of logs beneath us, he remained steadfast and cheerful.

In the confined space, I wriggled on to my side and propped up on to my elbow. In the triangle of moonlight coming through the tent's open end, I watched him. Asleep, he looked so peaceful and calm. He was shirtless and his skin was smooth and milky-white. How did he stay so pale in the relentless sun? His hand, splayed on his chest, rose and fell gently.

"Are you watching me, Edward Kemp?" Burn murmured without opening his eyes.

"No," I stuttered, flopped on to my back, and turned my head away.

"You were." Burn shifted his body up to mine.

Even though the night air was warm, he felt cold. I pulled a fur up.

"You're freezing."

Burn pushed it back down to our feet. "I'm hot," he said and placed his fingers on my neck as if to prove a point. They were cold. With his hand unmoving, he waited. For what? Permission? The contact sent a little buzz down my spine that brought a smidge of pleasure akin to driving fast over a humpback bridge: that nanosecond when your stomach turns is pure joy.

He slid his hand on to my chest and spread a palm over my heart. "One. Two. One. Two," he counted.

"Am I still alive?"

Burn applied a little pressure. "Yes."

"But only just," I joked.

"Yes, The Bad Thing has taken a liking to the boy from another planet."

"So, it seems, have you." Fuck, I hadn't intended to say that out loud.

"You flatter yourself, Edward. I find you rude, arrogant, and self-centred."

I took his hand off my chest. "Thanks."

"But I am drawn to you like a magnet." Burn placed his hand back over my heart. "It's beating faster." He was right. This boy was getting under my skin and I was allowing him. Burn and his bloody *spidey sense* knew that. I removed his hand, again.

"Tell me you do not enjoy the attention."

"I *don't* enjoy the attention."

"Then stop me." Burn slipped his hand along my collarbone and down the line of my ribs.

My body tensed and I dug my fingernails into the bedding. I didn't move until Burn's wandering hand reached just below my navel. Was I so desperate for attention, any attention, that I would accept his advances? I muttered a few incoherent words before giving him a brief glance, twisting around, and scrambling out of the tent.

He joined me on the shadowy bank. Even in the moonlight, Abaytor was impossibly dark. I'd learned, to my cost, to take a candle on any night-time loo trips. Burn, looking colourless under the full moon, waited for the showdown. Seconds ticked by. I shook my head and gazed at my feet. "Burn – please just take me to the Landing Plains."

"That is what I am doing, Edward."

"Yeah and the rest."

"Meaning?"

"This journey has turned into a bloody sightseeing trip. And you're hell bent on seducing me."

He laughed.

Swivelling towards him I growled, "I'm not interested," and then stalked past him.

Burn caught my arm and whispered, "Are you sure?"

I wasn't sure about anything any more. Wrenching away, I stamped back to the raft. My limbs ached and my eyes felt heavy. Pulling a fur up and over my head, I curled into a ball and buried my face in the pillow.

I was stark naked and lying on a log. Its rough bark jutted into my skin as I wrapped my arms around it. I'm sure I should have been cold, but I was hot, and confused thoughts tumbled through me like falling leaves. The river reared beneath me. I dug my fingernails in and hung on.

"Why were you naked?" Burn asked the next morning as I told him about the dream.

"Dunno, though it was probably something to do with you."

"Oh, I do hope so."

I was in no mood the following day, or the day after, for Burn's sightseeing trips. I pushed him to travel until the sun edged the horizon, and to set off again at first light.

I needed to go home, to feel cotton sheets on a bed that didn't move, to have a haircut, wear clean clothes, to drink proper tea and eat real food, to look at skyscrapers, cars and television. I wanted to be with people who didn't wear bows and arrows as fashion accessories, and have some privacy for *private* things. I was positive those things were more important than my father, his stupid bees, the collection of wood that called itself a raft, and the annoying native. I thought so, anyway.

Now and then, Burn would complain that we'd passed a famous site or an interesting village and I'd ignore him. Above all on my wish list, I was desperate to live without fear of The Bad Thing.

Instead of sitting on a barrel, I found a wide piece of driftwood and, much to Burn's amazement, fashioned a makeshift oar by tying it to a thin branch. Kneeling on the opposite side of Burn's poling, I pulled the oar through the water and each stroke took me closer to home.

Now, as I gawped at an endless lake of water in front of me, I knew that the time we'd gained would be lost. Why was it always one step forward and two steps back on this bloody planet?

"So what's its name?" Considering there was no Internet, Burn's encyclopaedic knowledge of his planet was staggering.

"Endilos Lake; it means endless."

I could see how it got its name. The broad sky above reflected in its glass-like surface as a perfect mirror image. There was no visible horizon to ground you, so as we entered the lake, I had a weird sensation of flying. My head spun, my stomach churned, and I retched.

"You will get used to it." Burn moved to the front of the raft, tipped his head back, and held his arms out wide. The famous scene from *Titanic* popped into my mind and I wasn't going to be his Jack.

The lake had a slight current and little wind, so the *Queen* idled on the surface. Dropping to my knees, I dug my oar into the reflections, sensing we were in for a long haul. Burn picked up his pole and stabbed it into the water. It stopped suddenly. He toppled backwards, jumped up, and cleared his throat. "The lake is shallower than it looks."

"That's good. Now you can push as I pull and we may make progress."

Five minutes later, Burn shouted, "Edward, you are pulling in the wrong direction."

"How the *fuck* do you know which direction to head in?" I swept my arm in an arc.

"We came out of the mouth of the river heading towards the sunrise. I know the river enters and exits this lake in a straight line. If we keep the sun in front of us in the morning and behind us in the afternoon, we will locate the river again."

The trouble was that Burn pushed harder than I pulled, which resulted in a comedic crab-like movement across the water. It got us nowhere fast. I sat back on my haunches, hurled the oar on to the deck, and exhaled noisily.

Ignoring my drama queen moment, Burn gazed across the endless water. "My father talked about this lake. He said it was a dreamland and the most magical thing he had ever seen."

Burn never talked about his father, or his mother. "That's the first time I've heard you mention him."

"Yes."

"Why?"

"He never really featured much in my life."

"Like mine, then."

"Yes. I was their much-wanted son, but I never lived up to my father's high expectations of me. I brought shame on him."

I stood to face him. "Burn, I'm sure you didn't."

"You are kind but I did. Some days, I considered tying rocks to my feet and ending it all in the river." With his pouting bottom lip and wide eyes, he looked six years old.

I didn't know what to do with that information. Should I mumble some kind words or ignore it? I went for the latter and instead said, "You know what, I think we may have troublesome fathers in common."

He looked up and grinned. "Maybe tonight, we can compare our experiences."

"Let's not go that far."

We paddled all morning and when the sun was at its blistering best, I dropped the oar and crawled under the shade of the canvas. Burn joined me, carrying water, and some odd-shaped nuts he'd picked up two days before. He shelled them between two stones and dropped them into a little wooden bowl. They tasted like pine with an aftertaste of furniture polish. I spat them out. "Burn, are you trying to poison me?"

"No!" His mouth fell open.

I sighed. "You know, I reckon we'll move faster if we pull the *Queen*. The water will only come up to our hips."

Burn slapped me on the back. "That is an excellent idea, Edward. We will take it in turns."

When the sun dipped behind the raft, he stripped to his waist and his pale skin glowed in the sunlight.

"Burn, how come you never, um, burn?"

He shrugged and dropped into the lake with a plop. I threw him a rope; he tied one end around a log, threw the other end over his shoulder, and heaved the raft forward. The *Queen* reared a little at the front and then settled into a gentle seesaw motion as he tugged her through the water.

Swapping places every so often ensured we progressed at a good pace for the rest of the day. As the light faded, I tied the rope to a large boulder on the lakebed, and clambered on to the deck.

We watched the sun drop into the lake and set our world on fire. The sky became shades of flaming orange and so too did the water. I was standing in Hell and it was the most awe-inspiring thing I'd ever seen, until it got dark. Then, the stars came out, and we became insignificant in the countless pinpricks of light that surrounded us. Closing my eyes, I let the image burn into my memory. I never wanted to forget it.

I looked at Burn, who was staring at me with a faraway look in his eyes. I could guess what was on his mind. It was always on Burn's mind. It was also on mine. The place demanded it and the lack of privacy wasn't helping my … urges. I went to bed. Alone.

The dawn brought with it a shock. Numerous floating houses circled us like wagon trains in old Westerns. They were round and built of mud and sticks with a thatched roof. They bobbed and spun on the lake surface like ballet dancers and seemed to have no visible support. Short people emerged from the raised arched doorways with tiny loincloths that only just hid their privates, and rows of what looked like finger bones curving around their bodies; I hoped to God they were fancy beads.

"This is not good," Burn croaked.

"Not good?" I repeated.

"The Canibra tribe. They do not like outsiders on their lake. And you cannot get any more *outside* than you."

"Fab. Now what?"

"We smile." Burn turned around on the spot so he could grin at every occupant of the round houses. I followed his example. In hushed tones Burn said, "The tribe are renowned for their bad temper and zero tolerance."

"That's great," I muttered.

A woman, fatter than the rest and with no top on, jumped into the water and waded over to the raft. The *Queen* complained under her weight as she clambered aboard. She faced me and lifted her arm. There was a whistling sound –

I awoke to stars floating in front of my eyes. I blinked to focus. We were lying on the wooden floor of one of the round houses, the door was shut, and we were alone. Burn was by my side, hands tied behind his back and feet tied together. He was out cold. My hands and feet were also tied; I flexed against the bonds and yelped. The twine had tiny barbs, and every movement dug them further into my skin. Burn stirred.

"Burn," I breathed.

"Um."

"What the bloody hell happened?"

He shook his head and focused on me. "My guess is she fired a dart which knocked us out."

"What do they want with us?"

"Sex slaves."

"You're joking!"

"Yes."

I swung a two-footed boot on to his shins. This was not the time for Burn's irritating jokes.

"Ow." Burn scowled at me before saying, "They may want to trade us for food or supplies."

"That's barbaric."

"To us, yes."

I'd adapted to the rolling movement of the raft, but the spinning of the house was making my stomach churn. "Let's get out of here." Before I could move, the door swung open.

A man entered and stood, feet apart, licking his lips.

"Let us go," Burn demanded.

"No." His voice was as harsh as a fifty-a-day smoker. He poked Burn in the stomach with his toe. "You are no good to me. But you ..." He turned and his mouth dropped open exposing rotting teeth. "You will do very nicely."

"For what?" I meant to say the words loud and with an air of authority but they came out as a squeak.

Dropping to his knees by my side, he leaned over and said, "For fun," and stroked my cheek and then let his fingers trail my throat.

"You can fuck right off!" I flapped on the floor like a stranded fish as I tried to move away from him. He shushed me, grabbed the waistband of my shorts, and pulled me into him. He smelt like a wet dog; I turned my face away. Burn wriggled so we were at right angles to each other and made a vain attempt to kick him with his tied feet. He laughed him off and never let his gaze leave my face. His strong fingers wrapped around the top of my shorts pushed further down. They were cold and rough as they traced the line of my hipbone.

"FUCK OFF!" I twisted away from him and propelled myself towards Burn.

He stood up and cackled like a witch as another man appeared in the doorway. "Leave them for now but, before the sun goes, dispose of this one," he said pointing at Burn. "This one." He nodded towards me. "Strip him and bring him to me."

They left the room, leaving the door ajar. Clearly, they didn't believe us to be a threat.

"Do you still have that flint in your bag?" I hissed at Burn.

"Yes."

"Come here."

Burn wriggled like a caterpillar over to me. He positioned himself so his bag, which hung at his navel, rested near my outstretched fingers. I shifted into his space and searched out the drawstring. Burn giggled.

"Stop it. Now is not the time." I knew my probing fingers would amuse him. Pulling the cord, I rummaged inside and withdrew the flint. "Flip over."

"I thought you would never ask."

"Burn! For fuck's sake, don't you care that by sundown I'll be that man's fodder?"

"Sorry." He turned so our bound hands were together. Positioning the flint with care, I hacked at the twine.

"Hurry," Burn urged.

"Nearly there. Hang on." The ties twanged apart and Burn leapt to his feet.

I stared at him. "You're not bleeding." Burn's wrists had twine marks but no blood.

Burn rubbed at the sore area. "No, it seems not."

"Why not?"

He shrugged, hauled me to my feet, and sliced the twine in one movement. I rubbed my wrists, smearing trails of blood up my arms, before heading towards a small window.

Secured to the back of the house by our towing rope was the *Queen*. She appeared to be undisturbed with our belongings where we left them. We crept to the door. Why was there no one guarding us? I peered through the open door. Only the lake and sky filled the gap. Where were the other houses? More importantly, where was the rotten-toothed man and his mate?

We took a step out and squinted into the sunlight. Our house drifted to the right as another dwelling floated into view. And there he stood, in its doorway, swinging in time to the motion of the house. He shrieked a war cry and leapt into the water. I recoiled and bundled Burn into action. A thin ledge, like the ones on narrow boats, ran around the house, except this one had no handrail. There was a whistling sound, I ducked and somehow missed a dart. Another high-pitched sound and Burn ducked. Jabbing our fingers into the mud side of the house, we bobbed and weaved our way around to the back. Screams and chants followed our progress as other voices joined that of the man's.

We leapt into the water as one. My limbs wouldn't work. It was like a dream where you want to run but can't. I exhaled a long held breath and forced myself to doggy-paddle. Burn was on the *Queen* before me. He clutched my T-shirt and hauled me aboard. As Burn cut the *Queen* free, the air was full of whistles and shouts. I swear Burn's gods were with us as we avoided the darts.

My arms ached and my chest felt like it would burst but, high on adrenaline, we paddled and poled away from the floating village. With no way of controlling their houses' speed, the hollering Canibra tribe were left behind in no time.

The Copper River had never looked so inviting. We heaved the *Queen* into the flow and collapsed into a breathless heap. For a long while, I listened to Burn's panting, and enjoyed the *Queen* rocking under me. I was grateful for them both.

Burn insisted on tending to my sore wrists. The medicine man in him loved a patient. I sat cross-legged on the deck and he mirrored me. A terrible smell of rotten eggs drifted into my nostrils. "Is that you?"

"No, it is not. It is the healing poultice." Burn nodded towards the shallow bowl in his hands. He scrapped his fingers around the edge and they emerged covered in pale grey goo. "Here, give me your wrists."

I duly did so.

Burn gripped my fingers with one hand, while applying the cold paste in slow circular motions with the other. "So, he wanted a piece of you."

"I don't want to talk about that man."

"The experience may have been pleasurable."

"Burn! You're sick."

"I am quite well."

"I wouldn't have let him have any of me."

"Good," Burn whispered.

An uncomfortable silence fell between us until I broke it with, "I see the food's gone."

"Yes, but we have our lives."

I nodded and then stuck out my bottom lip. "The wounds sting." Burn ignored me and applied the poultice to the other wrist. He then worked it down along my palms and on to my fingers. Taking a finger in turn, he slowly worked the slippery goo up and down and up and down. My fingers didn't need tending, but there was something hypnotic about the motion and something pleasurable about the sensation. When he'd finished working the right hand, he moved to the left. With each slippery finger, the tension released from my shoulders and I sagged a little until sleep took me.

Chapter Eleven

I awoke to a bright morning and found myself wrapped in one of the coarse blankets that Treater had donated to us. Without looking, I was aware that grey goo still smeared my hands; I crawled over to the edge of the raft and trailed them in the water.

"Morning," Burn's bright voice chirped from behind me.

Dropping my head on to the deck I moaned, "Is it?"

"Yes. Today is a good day. I know it."

"No Bad Thing?"

"No."

I shuddered. "No rotten-toothed man wanting a piece of my ass?"

"No."

"Good, I don't think my heart can take any more."

"Oh."

"Oh?"

Burn didn't have to say anything as he pointed into the near distance. I knew by the way his finger shook he wasn't pointing at a rainbow. My mind went into overdrive. I could submerge myself under the raft but how would I breathe? I could chuck water at it. With what? I scanned the deck: a barrel, too heavy; a crate, too holey.

Burn nudged my shoulder, pulling me from my frantic thoughts. "It is okay. It is only a shadow." He raised his eyebrows and smiled.

I slapped him around the head. "That's fucking great, Burn."

"Ow, was that necessary?"

"Totally."

He sat with a thump and rubbed his temples. "You have given me a headache."

"You scared me."

"Then, I am sorry."

I sat next to him and picked up his mortar – God only knew what it contained – but it looked like it needed a bashing, so I grabbed the pestle and pounded it into a pulp. Apart from the knocking of wood on wood, all was silent.

"I have remembered a story a wandering troubadour told me," Burn said on a rush of air. "The storyteller's name was Frederic, and he was my favourite."

I flashed him a look.

"No. Not in that way!"

I grinned.

"His tales were always about mystery and magic. One such tale was about a poor man called Cedric Crouch. It is a true story. Would you like to hear it?"

"Do I have to?"

"Yes." Burn took a deep breath. "One evening, at sunset, a humble man called Cedric Crouch was spear-fishing in a shadowy bend of the river. He aimed towards dots of light just under the water's surface, which he took to be eyes of the Tumbaga fish. The spear struck its quarry true and Cedric recoiled into the shallows. He tugged his prize on to the shore and nearly fainted at the sight. He had caught a fish which was as tall as a man and as black as night. This was strange, but the strangest thing about the fish was its flanks. On them, catching the dusky light, were thousands of water drops. Even when Cedric ran his hand along them, they never moved or lost their shape. Cedric was not as young as he once was and it took all his strength to heave the giant fish back to his settlement. The next morning, eager to show off his catch, Cedric hung the fish from the gallows in the market place for everyone to see –"

"You hang people?" I interrupted.

"Yes, Edward. Some tribes use hanging as a punishment."

"Permanent punishment? Does yours?"

"We used to, but not now. May I continue?"

I grunted a reply.

"The villagers muttered and poked the jewelled sides of the fish. They all agreed it was the most absurd creature they had ever seen. *Then* –"

Burn said the last word so loud I lurched.

He grinned and repeated, "– *then* the fish sighed. A breath of black vapour rushed out of its mouth and curled itself into a cloud. It darkened, grew, and consumed the fish and the gallows. People raced away, screaming. The sight terrified Cedric and rooted him to the spot. His terror was to become his downfall. The horror surrounded him in a deathly embrace.

"A girl collecting sweet-grass found the dry husk of his body two days later by the side of the river. That was the end of Cedric Crouch but the start of The Bad Thing that now stalks our planet."

I put the mortar and pestle down with a resounding thud and jumped up. "That can't be true. Monsters don't come from fish."

"Edward, because it is something you have never seen does not make it an untruth."

He was right, but nothing on this planet made sense. Its people believed in gods of rivers and fog monsters. My twenty-first century Earth brain knew these things to be the work of fantasy writers and sci-fi films. Burn accepted their existence without a second thought. With a sudden urge to lie down and escape his world of myths and bedtime stories, if only for a moment, I crawled under the canvas.

Burn inched in next to me and took up all the room, as usual.

"Do you have to?"

"What?"

"Follow me everywhere?"

Burn shrugged, as if it were a given that where I was, he was as well.

I wriggled away from him. "What do you want?"

"There is a settlement near here I would like to visit, and then I *promise* I will take you straight to your ship."

"Another? What's so special about this one?"

"It is Cedric Crouch's village."

"That was just a story."

Burn twisted on to his front and propped up on his elbows. He pressed his fingers to his lips and eyed me from under his overgrown fringe. "Please, Edward."

"Burn –"

"They have three-headed dogs."

"They do not."

"I can prove it."

I sagged. "Whatever."

He threw his arms around my neck and kissed my ear. I shoved him away. "You're mad." He left the tent humming the same irritating tune. I stroked the ear he'd kissed as if I were feeling it for the first time.

Burn poled the *Copper Queen* through an expanse of flat red plains. For ages, there were no undulations in the surface, apart from an occasional boulder, no trees, and no signs of wildlife. The air was hot and dry and there was a burnt newspaper smell like a car running hot. Really, if someone had told me we were on Mars, I would have believed them. These days, I would consider anything.

A bone-dry wind bothered the raft and coated everything in fine red sand. Sweeping the dust off my clothes, I noticed, not for the first time, how grubby I looked. My jeans were torn and filthy, red scratches marked my arms, my feet were bare, and God only knew what my hair was doing. I caught Burn watching me.

"You are lovely."

"Now, that's not true."

"The Edward Kemp who stepped on to my raft is not the same Edward Kemp who I see before me."

"No, he was clean and coiffured."

"And he was false."

I opened my mouth to protest but Burn cut in.

"Without your armour of styled hair and expensive clothes, all that is laid bare is the true Edward. And *he* is lovely."

Did all my friends hide behind material items and the latest gadget? Who among them didn't care for the trappings of modern life, but were too afraid to be themselves? There, on a rickety raft on another world, I resolved that once I'd got home, I'd step out from behind the designer labels and try to persuade my friends to do the same.

I smiled at Burn, the annoying native who owned nothing, but was happier than anyone I knew.

"You are blushing."

"I'm not." The burn in my cheeks said otherwise.

The river curved into a long S-shape and as we came around the last bend, Cedric's settlement stood proud in the empty landscape. The buildings looked like the ground had coughed them up. Grouped together in a haphazard fashion they were as red as the earth. All the dwellings were square, flat-sided, and topped with a domed roof. I stood on the edge of the raft with my toes curled around the logs and leaned out across the water to get a better look. Squinting to focus, I noticed the buildings had no ground-level doors, only wonky ladders that led to arched entrances in the domes.

"Why the hell did they settle in the middle of no-man's land?"

"Attackers have nowhere to hide. They can see them well before they reach the perimeter."

"Attackers?" I didn't like the sound of that.

"Cedric's people are at war with a neighbouring tribe over land rights. There are also large beasts that live in this area and, of course, The Bad Thing."

"What kind of beasts?"

"An ursus called the long-toed. They drag prey alive to their holes, pin it down and then they eat one limb at a time and leave the head till last."

"Bloody hell. Do they also have rotten-teethed men?"

"I do not know, Edward."

"I'm not leaving the *Queen*."

"Edward, it will be okay, not all tribes are like the Canibra. I will protect you."

Now I was worried.

We were spotted before we'd left the raft. A buttery shimmer came towards us across the open plain. Yellow saris, flapping in the breeze, draped the bronze bodies of several people. The leader was a muscle-strapped man with a bare upper body criss-crossed with battle scars, some still raw. He wore a plain gold circlet that rested on a mane of grey hair. He strutted at the head of the party, with everyone else keeping a careful step behind. Burn set off towards them. I hesitated. Were these people friendly or hostile? Were there any lurking long-toed ursus? Burn didn't seem to be worried, so like a faithful puppy I followed in his wake. We met somewhere half way between the settlement and the river.

No one spoke. Bloody telepaths. Burn's blank-eyed stare always freaked me out. I swung my arms, glanced over my shoulder to check for limb-loving beasts and sighed. My throat was parched and my head was baking. Then, I saw her. A Greek goddess, with hair as red as the earth, and the wrap of material she wore only just hiding her shapely body. She caught me goggling and smiled.

Burn put two fingers under my chin and closed my mouth. "The leader has invited us to a feast."

"Great," I said, only hearing every other word as I stared at the girl.

"I told them that, afterwards, you would tell them about your planet."

I heard that. "What? Like an after-dinner speech?"

"Yes."

"That's fab. Thanks."

"No problem, Edward."

I made a mental note to teach Burn about sarcasm.

"Who are they?"

"They are the Benuim, but after Cedric's story, they are also known as the Fish Breath people."

"You have got to be joking!"

"No, Edward, I am not."

I snorted. "Your people are brilliant at names."

"Thank you."

I guffawed. Burn scowled at me. "This," he pointed towards the leader, "is Kai, and the rest are his courtiers."

I composed myself and nodded towards Kai. He browsed my body and I could feel him scrabbling around in my head. I mentally closed doors and turned to face Burn. "And the girl?" I mouthed.

"His daughter." Burn squinted at me in the bright sunlight. "And I suggest you stay well away, Edward."

"Why?"

"By the interlocking rings she wears, she is to be hand-tied."

The party strolled back towards the settlement. To annoy Burn, I walked behind the girl and gawked at her swinging hips and ample backside.

"Stop it," Burn hissed.

I had the devil in me so I sidled over to him. "Come on, she is pleasing to the eye."

"I suppose so."

The question that had been playing on my lips for some time came blurting out. "Burn. Do you *do* girls?"

"Do?"

I danced a circle around him. "Are you, you know, *into* girls?"

"If I like someone, it does not matter if they are a boy or a girl."

"So, have you had a girlfriend?"

"No, Edward. I have not." Burn gave me a withering look, sidestepped away from me, and increased his pace.

Changing the subject, I called after him. "Why are the entrances so high off the ground?"

Burn stopped, scrubbed a hand over his face, and sighed. Sometimes, I felt I drove him to his limits. "They are to protect the people from invaders and beasts. But, of course they are no protection from The Bad Thing."

The ladders had seen better days due to the constant pulling in and dropping down. They didn't appear able to support my weight. Two led up to the same entrance, so I queued behind the girl and winked at Burn. What was I trying to prove? Was I trying to underline the fact that *I* was into girls? He shot me daggers and climbed his ladder to the roof. My ladder choice rewarded me with an eyeful of smooth long legs and wafts of spicy perfume.

Up high, I squinted into the distance. The shiny copper ribbon of the river coiled across the vast red plains that linked to the pale violet sky in a blur of heat. Hundreds of tiny black birds swirled in formation like shape-shifting starlings. I wished my mobile phone worked so I could capture the image, but the battery was flat so I closed my eyes and burned it to my memory instead.

Then I turned my attention to the centre of the buildings – a square courtyard held a bustling market. Spices the colour of fire were mounded high in wicker baskets, vivid glass lanterns glittering like jewels hung from every stall, and next to them intricately woven rugs flapped in the breeze waiting for Aladdin. People dressed in yellow flowed around the stalls like a custard river and in the middle, surrounded by respectful space, were the gallows from the story. It all looked very … foreign.

Stepping off an inside ladder, I stood next to Burn, who crossed his arms. "I've seen the gallows from Cedric's story."

Burn ignored me. He ignored me a lot. Maybe, that was the only way to deal with me.

The room was not how I'd imagined. I thought we'd be squatting on the ground around a miserable fire pit. Why had I not learnt to expect the unexpected by now? A heady smell of incense stung the back of my nose and dust motes swirled in beams of light coming from high windows. Colourful rugs covered the earth floor along with hundreds of floor cushions with a blue human-shaped pattern on them. I shivered. "Burn, what's with the blue man?"

Burn glanced over his shoulder. "What blue man?"

"I have seen that symbol before, in the Haruspex's pyramid." I nodded towards the cushions.

Burn looked at me as if I'd fallen off the silly wagon.

"I did." I resisted the urge to stamp my foot.

"Okay, Edward." He walked away.

Amongst the unsettling cushions were candles in gold mounts, placed on low wooden tables. In the middle was a palm tree, bent under the weight of trinkets hung from sparkling thread. But the most interesting feature in the room was the multiple rows of buckets suspended mid-air on a rope and pulley system. I had a good idea what they were for.

Circled around the palm were tables groaning under the weight of cheeses, meats, and flat breads. Around them stood waiting servants and, lining the room, many yellow-wrapped and blank-faced people leant against the walls.

I caught up with Burn and whispered in his ear. "Did they know we were coming?"

"Probably."

"Where are the dogs?"

"We can ask to see them after the feast." Burn's tone reminded me of my father dealing with me as a small boy constantly asking questions.

A servant, with wide eyes the colour of coal, hurried over with a bowl of black fruits. Burn took one and nodded his thanks. I copied and it squished between my fingers. I ate it and licked the juice that was running down my hand. It tasted of nothing and it certainly didn't fill me up so I couldn't see the point of them.

Kai pointed for us to sit. I scanned the room for his daughter and chose a cushion opposite her. Burn sat two cushions away. There was an irresistible aura around the girl. Like a moth to a flame, she drew me in. Tucking her long legs under her, she caught my gaze and smiled. I smiled back.

Burn leaned over and tapped my arm. "Stop ogling, Edward."

I groaned. "I'm not ogling. How do you even know that word?"

He ignored my question and fiddled with his hair. "Your attentions towards the girl are going to … get us into trouble."

"You're jealous!"

"I am not!"

"Oh, you are, too."

"I. Am. Not." He swivelled away from me and crossed his legs and arms.

Another servant handed me a plate loaded with meat and bread. I was hungry. Burn's idea of portion size was laughable. It was no wonder he was so skinny. Taking a large chunk of bread, I swooped up some meat and shoved it in all at once. It tasted of fire and spices and reminded me of my favourite Indian restaurant. I stuffed in more.

"What's the meat?" I spoke with my mouth full.

"Capra."

I choked. "Goat!"

The feasting lasted into the late afternoon. Apart from the shuffling of servants, the room was quiet. I presumed all the sparkling conversation was going on beyond my capabilities. After a dessert of foul-smelling cheese, washed down with gritty coffee, Kai indicated for me to stand. I glanced at Burn, who raised his eyebrows and flashed a grin. At that moment, I could have happily thumped him. Again.

What was I going to say? These people would have no understanding of my indulgent lifestyle. Clasping and unclasping my fingers, I stood and cleared my throat. "My name is Edward Kemp and I live on planet

Earth." Well, that sounded weird. "My father, Herb, discovered Abaytor and –" I stopped and scanned the room. The girl, with her hands in her lap and her lips parted, sat next to Kai, who was frowning at me. I needed Burn.

"Edward." He appeared at my side. Thank God. Facing the audience he said, "Edward's people are curious and inventive. They have strived for the unknown, be that in the stars or the ocean's depths, for many years. Herb Kemp, through conviction and bravery, realised his dream and found our planet."

It had never occurred to me that my father was brave.

"Now, Edward, think about Earth and they will see it in pictures."

I shut my eyes. *All I know is, when I look into Abaytor's skies, I see Earth, shining brighter. She is a star of snow-topped mountains and deep-blue oceans. She teems with life, from the birds in the sky to the fish in her seas and with her vast skies, huge moon, and endless light shows of sunset and sunrise she is a beauty to behold.* I opened my eyes to a sea of attentive bronze faces.

"Well done, Edward." Burn clapped me on the back.

Then the room erupted, unfortunately not in recognition of my speech.

The Bad Thing had seeped in unnoticed while all eyes were on me. It hung like a vaporous blanket above the bucket line. I wondered if it was a sentient being and aware of the water trap. Kai pushed through the throng and grasped the rope that activated the system. He waited.

Pressing my back against the wall, I held my breath. When I was a child, there was a game called Mr Wolf, where a group of us would creep up unnoticed on the kid who played the Wolf. He or she could, at any point, turn, chase us, and *eat* us. Well, that's what it felt like. Waiting and watching with my heart in my throat. Would The Bad Thing move first, or Kai, or – me? It had to be me; Burn believed an alien on Abaytor was irresistible to it.

I stepped into the middle of the room. I didn't know whether I wanted to impress the girl or prove to Burn I wasn't just a useless alien, or maybe I had just found a conscience. Whatever it was, I found myself looking into the depths of the beast.

"Edward? What are you doing?" Burn shrieked.

"Bait."

"No!" He lurched for me.

There was no time for him to pull me back before The Bad Thing enveloped my body. Weeping, I dropped to the floor. The urge to call it a day, give in, and submit was utterly compelling. I was no one important. My fuddled brain decided that if the Bad Thing didn't kill me then I would. A rapid plan formed, I would use one of Burn's knifes and slit my wrists. I'd heard it was the most certain way of committing suicide.

A deluge of water cascaded on to me and flooded around my knees. I swept it away with my hands. I wanted to die. But the water had the desired effect. The black terror shrivelled, and I was born-again as it twisted into a long thin shape and slithered out of a window.

Arms wrapped around my crouching form and Burn's head burrowed into my neck. "Do not do that again."

"I'll try not to." I grabbed his arms and held on. "I was going to end it all, Burn."

"Do not do that either." He helped me up and I leaned on him as we surveyed the drenched room.

Kai approached and held out his hand. "Thank you."

I shook it and then whispered to Burn. "Zero to hero."

The leader gathered up two soggy cushions. "The buckets are a temporary solution. We need a permanent one. I am responsible for that because one of my subjects released the horror. There is a rumour that if The Bad Thing can be captured in a metal-lined box, then it will blow itself out in fury." He nodded, spun on his heels, and joined a huddle of muttering people.

While Burn was helping with the clear up, I snuck over to the girl. Wet, she looked incredible – the fabric clung to her curves and strands of hair wound over her shoulders. It had been a while and certain urges overtook rational thought. Placing my hand on her lower back, I guided her towards a drier, and dimmer, corner of the room.

We stood within a breath of each other. "Hello, I'm Edward."

"I know." She smiled and placed her hand on my cheek.

A shudder vibrated through me. Raising my hand to hers, I interlaced our fingers. "Listen, I wondered if –"

I don't remember how I came to be on the floor with a red-faced brute of a man stood across me. Then Burn's legs straddled my shoulders, resulting in a view of Burn I never thought I'd see. He attempted to calm the man down with soothing hand gestures and cooing noises. He looked down between his legs. "Edward, this is Able – the intended."

Fuck.

"Unfortunately he wants to kill you."

Fuck.

Burn yanked me up and manhandled me behind his back. We sidestepped towards the ladder; all the while Burn maintained eye contact with the outraged Able whose arms were been constrained by two other men – but he wrenched free. Burn's breathing was loud and I could feel his heart beating on my chest. "Run, Edward." He shoved me across the room.

Dodging around confused courtiers, we scrambled up one ladder and skittered down the other. As we pelted away from the settlement, we heard Able yelling from the rooftop, "Release the hounds!"

Burn sprinted to my side. "You know you were questioning the whereabouts of the three-headed dogs?"

"Yes."

"You will find that they are behind you."

I glanced over my shoulder. Two bodies and six snarling heads, half leapt and half fell down the ladders.

"Holy *fuck*. Run."

"Hero to zero!"

"Yeah, thanks, Burn."

Keeping ahead of the pack, I risked a glance and regretted it. Six snapping mouths with rows of long teeth filled my vision and Burn's high-pitched yelps filled my ears.

With the dogs nipping at our heels, we only just managed to hurtle on to the *Queen* and shove her into the flow of the river. I wiped the sweat out of my eyes and looked back. The freaks of nature were running along the bank and Able was not far behind them. Burn rammed the pole into the riverbed, the *Queen* reared and shot forward.

When the dogs and Able were dots in the distance, Burn dropped on to the deck panting. "We were lucky to get away with our lives. Could you not control your urges?"

I pouted. "It's been a while."

"For you and for me."

"Yes, and you want *it* with me."

"Do not flatter yourself. Your actions today were idiotic."

He was right. I'd overstepped the mark and become a self-absorbed alien crashing into a culture I didn't understand.

"Yes. I agree. I shouldn't have tried to take advantage of an innocent girl."

"Pah! She knew exactly what she was doing. She wanted a piece of alien ass."

"Burn!"

He scrabbled around in a crate and hoisted a glass bottle high into the air. Even at dusk, the luminescent liquid it contained was vivid. "I need a drink."

"You stole that from Naylor!"

"I borrowed it." He poured the mash into two small vessels and poked one into my hand.

"You're a bad influence."

"You are no saint. What is that delicious Earth saying – bottoms up?" Burn downed the mash in one greedy gulp.

The moon, low in the sky, peered out through a tear in a solitary cloud. Out of the billion stars now showing their faces, one shone brighter than the rest – home.

"More?"

I regarded the remaining liquid for a second before downing it in one. The mash burnt its way through my insides, then set fire to my belly. Spluttering, I squeezed my eyes shut and opened them again to a blurry vision of Burn topping up my cup. "Burn, are you trying to get me drunk?"

"Maybe." He winked.

"You act as if butter wouldn't melt, but you are pure evil."

He laughed, downed his second mash, swayed, and dropped. Even though he was flat on the deck in a star formation, he still managed to reach up, grab my trouser leg, and pull me down.

"Drink," he urged and pointed towards my full cup. The second hit of mash travelled cooler than the first and a comforting glow surrounded me.

I stretched out next to him and placed my hands behind my head. "No touching."

With mock horror in his voice, Burn replied, "Edward! Do you not trust me?"

"Nope."

He shrugged. I don't think he trusted himself. He inched up. "Your planet," he pointed with a wobbly finger in Earth's general direction, "is in the constellation of Many-many. It is the largest star gathering in our skies."

"Many-many? That's a crap name." They really were unimaginative when it came to names.

"Thank you."

I rolled my neck and groaned. The night sky had now burst into life and I was so small and – adrift. "When I'm home, where do I look to find you?"

"Abaytor is to the left of your North Star. Just below the cluster named Lyra."

"How the *hell* do you know that?"

"Herb told me."

"Oh. So how do I find Lyra?"

"Ask your pilot when you see him, he will tell you. Edward –" Burn stopped and propped up on to his elbows. He gazed at me through droopy eyelids.

"What?"

"Will you wave to me from time to time?" He slurred the words together.

"Um, yes." I had a sudden feeling of disorientation and ached for home. But – did I also want to stay? With Burn? I shook my head.

"Good." Burn got to his feet, hopped on one foot, swept up the mash bottle, and gulped the firewater.

Feeling more than a little unsteady myself, I stood up and grabbed the bottle from him. "Burn, you've had enough."

"Do you care about my wellbeing, Edward Kemp?" He snatched it back.

"No. Drink yourself into oblivion." I threw my hands into the air and turned away from him.

"Are you worried?"

I faced him. "About what?"

He swept a stray hair away and took a teetering step forward. He stared at me. "Are you worried I will seduce you? Or that you will succumb?"

Silence.

"You are! Remember to keep those mind doors closed, Edward."

I shoved him away.

He tripped, fell on to the deck, and lay in a crumpled heap. Bloody hell. A few heartbeats passed before he pushed himself up on to his hands and then leapt to his feet. He swung an angry fist around in a wide arc and missed me. Catching his flailing arms, I rammed them up behind his back and pinned them in place. He kicked out like an unbroken mule. The *Queen* rocked and complained under us. After a few bungled attempts, I hooked my ankle around his foot and pulled it from under him. He went down, and I fell on top of him. My front ran the length of his back and my heavier build pinned him to the deck. Burn bucked and reared in an effort to dislodge me.

"Get off." His shoulders twisted as his feet pummelled.

I rested my head into the nape of his neck. He smelt of fresh air and spices and his skin was cool and damp. My hipbones jutted into his lower back and the same little buzz vibrated in my stomach.

Burn stilled and his panting tailed off until he was silent. I breathed into his ear. "Hey, I thought you'd want me on top of you."

He dropped his forehead on to the deck with a whack. "Your positioning with its dominant seizing of my hands is *exactly* what I would have in mind."

I laughed and relaxed my grip.

"But you are crushing me, Edward."

I released him and slid to his side. Burn twisted on to his back and groaned. He rubbed, first his wrists and then his head. "I feel like Bacchus, the god of pain, has consumed me."

"Serves you right."

"Please, Edward, fetch my medicine crate."

"Nope." I grinned at him.

"You are cruel, Edward Kemp." He crawled across the deck.

"Oh, for God's sake. I'll fetch it." I found the crate and picked up a glass phial with mud brown liquid in it. "This one?"

"Yes. How did you know?"

"I can learn. Sometimes. Sit up."

Burn sat and dropped his head to his chest. The stopper came out of the phial with a loud pop. I lifted his chin. "Open wide." No response. I shook his shoulders. "Burn?" Nothing. I hoped he was asleep and not dead. "Burn?"

"Um?" He flicked his eyes open, then shut them again.

Placing the tonic to his mouth I whispered, "Here comes the train." His lips remained sealed. Sod it. I pushed him over and covered him with a blanket. As his snoring filled the night, I considered rolling him overboard. But, luckily for Burn, I fell into a mash-induced sleep.

I was stark naked and lying on a log. Its rough bark jutted into my skin as I wrapped my arms around it. I'm sure I should have been cold, but I was hot, and confused thoughts tumbled through me like falling leaves. Black growling clouds hung low and torrential rain stung my exposed skin. The wind-whipped river reared beneath me. I dug my fingernails in and hung on.

What the hell was happening? I had no memory of how I got here or why I had no clothes on. Where was the Queen? Was the log I was riding part of her? And where was Burn?

The log sailed the high water and with a bone-jarring smack, hit the dips. I lifted my head and adjusted my position. First mistake. The log spun and I rolled off into the biting water. I flung my arms back over it and hauled myself up. I now lay diagonally, with my arse in the air.

"Edward!"

Burn. Thank God. I twisted my head, and found him behind me, clinging on to a smaller log, bare-chested, and grinning.

"Nice view."

I awoke to the unmistakable sound of my father's cataraft filling the morning air.

Chapter Twelve

Bleary eyed, I crawled over to Burn and shook him.

"Go away, Edward," Burn mumbled from under the blanket.

I put my mouth near his ear. "You wouldn't be saying that if I was naked."

Burn scrambled upright. "Are you?"

"Nope."

He burrowed back down. "Go away, then."

"Charming." I paused. "My father's here."

Burn peered out from under the blanket. "Fuck."

"I couldn't have said it better myself."

My father's vessel pulled alongside the *Queen*. It was like when I camped in the garden as a kid and he would pop in at bedtime with cocoa, spoiling the illusion of adventure and the joy of freedom.

"Edward."

"Father."

"So, not at the Landing Plains yet?"

"Nope." Talk about stating the bleeding obvious.

He stood on the deck of his cataraft, wobbling from foot to foot. It was clear I'd inherited my lack of sea legs from him. His constant companion, Naylor, sat behind him smoking a long clay pipe.

"What have you been doing all this time?"

"Well." I took a long breath. "I've been half-drowned, half-starved, brain-probed, stalked by a fish-breath monster, suicidal, and terrified for my life. Oh, and we've done a bit of sightseeing along the way."

He stared at me, slack-jawed and wide-eyed. Naylor glanced up from his pipe.

"And." I pointed behind me to where I knew Burn was standing. "Did I mention my native guide is hell-bent on seducing me?"

Everyone stood in silence. Burn shuffled his feet on the log deck and Naylor sucked his pipe. I heaved a sigh and my shoulders sagged. "What do you want, Father?"

"We didn't expect to see you." He turned to Naylor who sat silent and puffing. "We thought you'd be on your way home by now." Then he faced me. "After a long trek, we found the cataraft moored where you'd left her." He waved a hand over the *Queen*. "I thought you'd have taken it instead of this. It would've gotten you to your ship faster."

Bloody hell. We'd shared the same space on the planet for two minutes and he was already questioning my choices. Plus, was he that desperate to get rid of me? I glared at him. "So what are you doing this far down the river?"

"Naylor and I," he paused. "We thought we'd have a little trip of our own."

"Aren't you supposed to be studying bees or something?"

"Yes. But I wanted some, um, down time." His cheeks coloured as he glanced at Naylor.

Ha, I was fucking right; they were doing the horizontal tango. I opened my mouth to make some inappropriate comment but Burn, like a bloody spectre, appeared in front of me and held out a long hand. "Come and break the fast with us. We can tell you all about our adventures."

"Burn. No."

"Edward. It is just breakfast." He winked at me. "It is not like we are asking them to share our bed."

"We are *not* sharing a bed!"

My father stepped next to me and stooped to peer under the canvas. The messy pile of furs and blankets gave no sign of two separate sleeping areas. "There appears to be only one bed to me."

"Father!"

He grinned and helped Naylor aboard.

I wanted him out of my life. Rooted to the spot, my head banged with thoughts. I'll demand that he leave. That'll cause a scene. I don't care. We can finish breakfast and then I'll send them on their way. That seemed the best option until my father sidled up and placed his mouth near my ear.

"So did he manage it?"

"What?"

"Burn. Did he manage to – win you over?"

"No, he *fucking* didn't! I'm obviously not easy like you!"

My father bellowed a raucous laugh and shoved me on the shoulder. "Don't mock it till you try it, son."

Before I could open my mouth to tell him to sod off, Burn gripped my wrist and whisked me to the other side of the raft.

He clapped his hands and did a little dance. "Look what Naylor has gifted me!"

"What?"

He pointed towards his feet. "A stove."

I wouldn't have called the over-large bean can with a drainpipe chimney, a stove.

"I can cook honey barms."

"Burn, that'll take ages. I want to go."

"You want to be rid of your father."

"Yes, that as well."

"Relax, Edward. Maybe you could talk to your father?"

"Talk to him? What about?"

"His quest for Abaytor."

I stalked off.

In the welcome cool of a cloudy morning, I sat next to my father and ate singed barm cakes. In silence. Again.

"You are approaching the Basin of the Descendants." Naylor broke the silence. There was no lead up to this announcement, unless he had been 'head chatting' with Burn. "It is a dangerous place. You will need extra eyes and ears as you travel through. I suggest we escort you to the other side."

"We can manage." The urge to rid myself of my father was stronger than any possible threat. I glanced sideways at Burn and repeated in my mind, *Don't agree, don't agree, don't agree.* What happened next scored high on the shock-o-meter. Burn cocked his head and frowned. Then, his voice vibrated around the inside of my skull like a marble in a jar, *Edward, I knew you had it in you.*

I jumped up and squealed like a little girl. The plate and burnt bits of honey barm skittered across the deck. My hand flew to my heart and then to my stomach, I didn't know whether I was going to have a heart attack or throw up. All the time I never took my eyes off him. "I heard you. I fucking *heard* you."

"And I you."

I turned to Naylor. "Did you hear me?"

"No, Edward, it seems you have developed a telepathic connection with Burn."

Developed? I didn't want to develop anything, especially with Burn. *How lovely. We have a connection.*

"Burn, fuck off out of my head." The boy was winning and I never lost at anything. I'd allowed him to caress me, steal my thoughts and wander through my mind. And he was always the focus of my suggestive dreams. He'd got so far under my skin that he had me searching for answers to questions I didn't know I had. There was nowhere to run, and now there was nowhere to hide.

"Relax, Edward."

I swear if he tells me to relax one more time on this trip, I will tie him to a tree and abandon him to the limb-loving ursus.

I would allow you to tie me to anything. Naked, of course.

"Fuck *off.*"

"Okay, Edward, I will behave."

My father coughed. "When you've both finished, I suggest we get underway. The weather is closing in."

"We? I never agreed."

It seemed my agreement was not called for. The three of them busied themselves in preparations whilst I stood, arms crossed, silent and sullen. Burn ambled past and flashed his eyebrows. He had the upper hand and it was hateful so I resolved to be as difficult as possible.

A cloud blanket hung low and threatening as Burn poled the raft through swelling waters. Why was everyone on board the *Queen*? Why was the cataraft dancing on the end of a rope behind her? I didn't ask. I sat with my back to them and sulked like a two year old.

A smell of pipe smoke mixed with spices wafted past my nose. Naylor. The elder sat down so close his knee dropped into my lap. He stared at me so I squeezed my eyes shut to try to keep the space invader from becoming a brain invader.

He laughed. "I am not here to steal your thoughts, Edward."

"Then why are you here?"

He nodded in Burn's direction. "I thought you would like to know more about him."

"What gave you that idea?"

He shrugged. "Burn did not have a good relationship with his father, either. That set him apart somehow. He did not make friends easily."

"That's because he's so irritating."

"Burn's restless spirit was never in the Fire Glade. It was as if it was waiting for something – or someone."

"Which isn't me."

"You act so indifferent to life, Edward. Learn to embrace what, and who, is around you."

"Don't tell me how to behave, Naylor." I shifted away from him and fiddled with the laces on my tatty sneakers. Nobody told me what to do.

"You need Burn to fill a space you did not know existed. And vice versa."

That was too deep for me. "I don't *need* him. He is my guide. That's all."

"You are destined to be together."

"Like Arthur and Merlin?"

"What?"

I shook my head. I wasn't about to explain British legends to a tribal elder on another planet.

Naylor moved closer. What was it with these people? "Burn also suffers from rejection issues."

"Also? I don't have *rejection issues*. What does that even mean?"

"You keep everyone at arm's length, Edward."

I do. It was the easiest option. That way there was no chance of getting hurt. But I said, "I don't." Of course, Naylor knew I was lying.

"Burn sees in you a kindred spirit and –" his eyes shone "– a cute arse."

"Oh. My. God. Naylor!"

For the first time his craggy face cracked a smile as he made to move. I placed a hand on his arm and stopped him. "So, what's this Basin place?"

"The stories say that the Basin of Descendants is the Underworld's waiting room. Those who have committed sin churn in a swirl of spirit soup while they wait for demons to open the doors. Then the Nether sucks the poor souls in like the wind snuffs out a candle."

"Great Halloween story."

"It is no story, young Edward. The Basin has taken Travellers before their time."

"What utter, *utter* codswallop."

Naylor scowled at me. "Sometimes, I do not know what Burn sees in you."

"My alluring charm? My boyish good looks?"

He stood, and without a word strode away. Bloody hell. Why was I so off with him? I liked him and felt drawn to his uncomplicated nature and serenity. It's just that underworlds, demons and ghouls don't exist unless you are thirteen and into *Twilight*. I stood, shoved my hands deep into my pockets, and sidled over to Burn. "I think I've pissed off Naylor."

"It does not surprise me, but I think we have more problems than that."

I looked in the direction he was staring and shuddered. The river had eaten into the earth and thrown up high rocky sides. In a windless sky, a huge black vaporous cloud churned. A metal taste coated my tongue. I stuck it out and made a face.

We approached the valley with all four of us standing in a line on the bow of the *Queen*. We squinted into the distance. The river, undecided on which course it wanted to take, looped through the steep sided valley.

As we neared the Basin, there was a rotten smell, like a bin that needed emptying, and the hairs rose on the back of my neck. You could cut the tension with a knife. Burn toyed with his pendant as Naylor made a strange *tsk* noise. My father was quiet as he half-heartedly pushed the pole into the water.

The walls of the valley flared, curved round, and narrowed again. This left the river to hug one side of the huge bowl and a desolate rock-strewn land to fill the other. As we entered the Basin, everything changed.

The high sides transformed from reddish-brown and bare-faced, to algae-smeared and dripping with stinking water. Vines draped their surface like thick green locks of hair and an ominous mist wound through them. There was a smell of decay in the air. I covered my mouth and nose for fear of retching. The mist clung to my skin and stuck my fringe to my forehead. I shivered. Then there were the sounds – eerie whistles like the wind through a keyhole and a faint chatter. Voices? A breeze through the trees? There were no trees. And I swear my over-active imagination heard the creak of a door.

Even the river seemed to quicken its pace. I glanced at the others. Burn was clutching his stomach as if in pain and Naylor had his eyes shut. My father was staring straight ahead; I knew he was wishing the *Queen* through the Basin because that's what I was doing.

"If The Bad Thing lived anywhere, it would be here," Burn whispered.

"Burn! You've jinxed it now!" As I said the words, a shadow flicked in the corner of my eye. I spun round. "What was that?"

"What?" three voices chorused.

"Something moved."

"Your imagination, Edward." My father picked up the push pole.

"It wasn't. I saw something."

"We've all worked ourselves up unnecessarily." He dug the pole into the water. "We'll be out of here in no time."

I scooped up my oar and knelt at the front of the *Queen*. As I paddled, I scanned the walls of the Basin for any movement, anything untoward.

The looming blanket of cloud fulfilled its threat and it poured the kind of rain that chills you to the core. A wind churned above our heads and whipped up tiny white horses on the river's surface.

Burn sat beside me. His hair stuck to his face and tiny droplets balanced on his long eyelashes.

"You are staring, Edward."

"I'm not!" But I had noticed how his sopping clothing outlined his lean torso.

Burn swivelled up on to his hands and knees and crawled over to place his mouth near my ear. "You were."

"Why would I stare at a skinny alien boy?"

Burn placed his mouth closer and murmured, "You tell me."

Despite myself, I grinned. Then, I spotted my father staring at us with half a smile on his lips. I shoved Burn away just as the *Queen* squealed and rammed to a halt. "What the fuck?"

"She has run aground." Burn crawled along the edge of the raft searching for the obstacle.

"Oh."

"Oh?"

"A large ring is jamming her underside."

"What?" I peered under the raft. Lying flat on the riverbed was a metal ring seated in a square mount, surrounded by shifting pebbles.

"It is a door handle."

"Burn. It's not a door handle. It'll be some kind of ancient mooring ring." He ignored my words as he scrambled backwards on all fours muttering under his breath. My father and Naylor knelt by my side. The raft complained under the weight and dug herself in further. They peered into the water.

"Someone is going to have to get in and free her, and since we are all soaked to the bone I don't think it matters who." My father rubbed the back of his neck. He would always do that when he had a problem.

Naylor and Burn shook their heads as one. I sighed, and without a word, slipped into the freezing water. The cold shot up my spine, forcing me to pull a sharp intake of breath.

"Be careful, Edward."

"Burn, it's not a door to the underworld."

Another shadow in the corner of my eye drove me to spin on the spot. With my feet unsteady on the pebbles, I toppled into the water and went under. It was as black as night. Why was it so dark when I could've only been a body's length under?

I surfaced into chaos.

The Bad Thing was hovering over my father, changing its shape every couple of seconds. A snake. A winged beast. A hula hoop? It shifted into a mass with hundreds of squirming tentacles. My father screamed as the feelers enveloped him. The Bad Thing lifted him, arms first and legs spinning, into its belly. I froze like someone had glued my feet to the floor. Naylor came into view; he scooped up a handful of cold water and chucked it in my face. "Edward, we need to assist your father."

My body released. I leapt on board the raft and yelled for Burn.

"On it!" He raced towards me with his bean can stove filled with water. I grabbed it and hurled its contents at the monster.

"Again!" I chucked the can to Burn who refilled it within the blink of an eye. There was no change after the second deluge. I hoped to God it wasn't becoming resistant because I knew from bitter experience my father didn't have long. Despite our differences, I didn't want to lose him. I loved him. "AGAIN!" Burn filled and I threw another four times before it shrivelled and relinquished its prize. My father fell to the deck and lay unmoving. "Father." I ran to him, dropped to my knees, and cradled his head. His hair was greyer and his face carried a few more lines. "Father?"

"Edward."

He was alive. I held him closer and rocked on my heels. "I thought I'd lost you."

"I'm … a tough … old chap," he mumbled.

"Are you okay?"

"I think so. Edward, it's terrifying in its grip … I felt like I was drawing my last breath."

"I was suicidal."

"It's taken you?"

"Yes, a few times. Burn says it has a taste for alien."

"Oh, Edward, I should have been there for you." He made to get up but I held him down.

"Stay there, you need time."

"All my wrongdoings came back to haunt me."

"Try not to talk. I'll get you some water." I indicated to Burn.

"I saw the people I used and left by the wayside in my blinkered drive for Abaytor."

Burn handed me a beaker of water. I smiled my thanks and held it to my father's lips. He placed his hand over mine and took a few sips.

"And I saw your small face at the window as once again I left you."

"You're left with terrible regrets after a Bad Thing attack. Don't worry, they'll pass."

"Maybe it's done me a favour." He made to get up, again. I gently held his shoulders.

"Burn and I have found a temporary solution *and* we have a plan –"

"A plan?" Burn interrupted.

"Yes. We are going to find a metal lined box and lure it in."

"We are?"

"Yes. Someone has to stop it. Once and for all."

"Excuse me, what have you done with Edward Kemp?"

"Naylor, look after my father. The *Queen* still needs releasing."

Naylor covered my father with a blanket as I strode over to Burn. "Once I free her, if you push-pole like your life depends on it and I paddle, we can get out of this hellhole sooner rather than later."

You are so sexy at this moment. He quivered and rolled an *mmmm* sound in his throat.

"Burn. Get out of my head!"

I like being – in you.

You're fucking incorrigible. And irritating. And – and a sex pest.

Burn laughed. I held back a snigger. He had a wicked and infectious sense of humour, but I wasn't going to let him see that I enjoyed his wit; it would make him far too big-headed.

For a second time, I dropped into the water and patted around under the raft until my fingers touched the ring. It was icy cold and I'm sure it vibrated. Pulling my hand away, I shouldered the log deck of the raft. She remained stuck fast. I placed both hands on her deck, buried my feet into the pebble riverbed, and heaved. Nothing.

"Burn and Naylor, you're going to have to jump off. It's too heavy."

"In there?" Naylor pointed at the water.

"Yes, in here and the sooner, the better."

Burn dropped in next to me with a soft slap.

"Naylor?"

"No." He shook his head.

"There is nothing here. Look." I swept my hand through the water and lifted a palm full.

Naylor crossed his arms and turned his head away from me. I sighed. "Okay, just you and me then, Burn." Two pairs of hands gripped the *Queen's* deck and heaved. Nothing. We dug our feet in and heaved again. The logs screeched in protest before the raft floated free. Then the silence fell, the wind paused, the surface of the river smoothed, and the mist vanished.

And the ring twisted.

Holy *fuck*.

We moved as one. A tangle of arms and legs dived on to the raft.

Someone yelled, "Paddle!"

I whipped up the oar, dropped to my knees, stuck it into the water, and pulled. A circular wind whipped around us, as if God was stirring the Basin with a spoon.

"The descendants are leaving," Naylor shouted.

"Get a grip, Naylor. It's just a wind." That said, something wasn't right. Time seemed to slow and it didn't matter how much I paddled, the raft stayed in the same place. My arms ached and fear sat heavy in my stomach. I gave the oar everything I had. As the raft suddenly released, we floated higher and sailed faster resulting in the *Queen* being spat out of the Basin.

"The ring turned." Burn's face was whiter than pale.

"It must have been the water's distortion," my father reasoned.

Naylor shook his head. "I saw it turn."

"I believe we all saw what we expected to see."

"It turned," Burn grumbled and steered the *Queen* towards a shallow inlet.

Was it a handle? Did we imagine it turning? Or, was it a watery illusion? I dropped to my father's side.

He took my hand. "You are brave. I've seen a different Edward today."

I shrugged. "It was nothing."

"Something has changed in you for the better. Is it the boy?"

"Burn? You did shove me on a raft with him for – I've lost count of how many days. Something was bound to have rubbed off."

"Will you miss him when you leave?"

I glanced at my annoying companion. "Miss him? He's an irritating space-and-brain-invader who doesn't take no for an answer."

"So you *will* miss him?"

"No." I was desperate for the comforts of home, but something was stirring in me – an energy, a spark, some kind of oomph. My unthinking reaction was to say 'no' but I could've just as easily said 'yes'.

"Anyway, it's clear I get my bravery from you." I smiled at him. Where had that sudden generosity come from?

My father's mouth dropped open. "You think I'm brave?"

"I didn't, but my time on Abaytor has made me realise that when you boarded the *Wave Rider* for the first time, bravery was the only thing you had."

He smiled and we sat in silence for a moment before he cupped my face. "You have your mother's eyes. She would have been proud of you today."

The world seemed to slow down as my father pulled me into an embrace. I went willingly and dropped my head on to his shoulder. I was bone-weary and drained. I sobbed into his neck. He held me and cooed into my ear. When I was a child, if I'd had a bad dream, I would slip into my parents' bed and feel safe. At this moment, in my father's arms, I felt safe.

But, it didn't last.

"I like this Edward," my father said.

"What do you mean?"

"I just meant you've changed for the better, that's all."

"There was nothing wrong with me before."

"You can be painful, son," he said – hurriedly adding, "as can I."

I wrenched away from him. "Painful? That's wonderful."

"Edward, don't be like that. I just meant –" He sighed. "I don't know what I meant."

"So you like me today, but not yesterday."

"I didn't say that."

"That's what you implied."

"You're twisting my words."

"Did you ever love me?" Talk about putting a cat amongst the pigeons.

"Of course I do."

"I never felt it. I spent my whole childhood with an absent father. And when you were around, your head was so full of star charts and ship-building that you had no time for me."

"Edward. Why don't you understand what I have achieved? I answered the question that's been on human lips since the dawn of time. I found an inhabited planet and proved that we are not alone."

"And you don't understand that I didn't care. You could have been the President of the United States or invented the *Walkman* or been Madonna's fuck buddy."

"Edward!"

I ran a hand through my hair. "I wanted a normal father – someone to kick a football with, someone who'd sit on the floor and eat pizza, or play *Super Mario Kart*."

"I'm sorry, boy. I was forced to make sacrifices."

Calling me *boy* really wound me up. I stood. "So I was the sacrificial offering to Abaytor?"

"No! Not at all. They are your words, Edward, not mine. Why couldn't you have been like your mother? She embraced celebrity and stood by me through thick and thin."

"Are you sure about that?" Heat flushed through my body. "Your bravery impressed me; I must have had blinkers on. You are selfish and always have been. I want you to leave."

"Edward, please, don't let these few cross words alter what we have."

I wasn't listening. I even hummed a tune in my head to block out his words. "Naylor. Help him up."

"Edward! Burn, please talk to him."

Burn held up his hands. "He will not listen to me, Mr Kemp."

"You have more influence over him than you know."

"What's that supposed to mean?" I shouted.

My father was now on his knees. "I've seen the looks you give him. If I knew you better, son, I'd say you've found more on this planet then you bargained for."

My fist struck his face before my brain engaged. He smacked the deck. I leant forward for another blow, but Burn gripped my arms and yanked me back. I was stronger than the skinny native and could wrench away at any point but I knew I needed him to control me.

Tears welled and my vision blurred as my father stood, wobbled, and massaged his reddening jaw. He glared at me, his brows met in the middle and his eyes were equally wet. "Did I strike a chord there, boy?"

I yelled, "NO!" at the top of my voice to drown out the nagging voice that was saying *yes*.

Naylor slung my father's arm around his shoulder and guided him away from me. "I think it is time we left. You need rest and I do not think you will get it here." My father didn't argue.

I held my hands up, jumped off the raft, and stormed off.

From a distance, I watched Naylor help my father climb into the cataraft. He didn't look at me as they sped down river. Why weren't they heading back to the Fire Glade so my father could complete his precious work?

Burn appeared by my side. "Some things are too broken to be fixed. However hard we try. Maybe you should accept that." He slipped an arm around my shoulder.

I shrugged it off and hugged myself. I could feel every rib. "I have to sleep."

Under the tangled ball of bedding, I stared at the dirty canvas roof. The *Queen* rocked gently under me and I could hear Burn humming as he went about his chores. I closed my eyes.

Searching fingers slipped under the hem of my shirt. My skin prickled to the touch. I trembled. Burn rolled a low sound in his throat and spread an open palm across my lower back. He yanked me into him. My body ran the length of his. I could feel his heart beating on my chest and his breath hot on my neck. He knitted the fingers of his spare hand with mine and pinned my arm up my back. Then, he hooked a foot around my ankle and pulled my legs apart. He placed his thigh between mine.

He'd claimed me. I'd allowed it. He'd won.

If Burn let me go, I would have dropped to the ground. He could sense my surrender and it fuelled his urgency. The hot hand pressing into my back slid down and under the waistband of my trousers. At the same time, hungry lips met mine.

I stopped breathing.

His exploring tongue took full ownership of my mouth as wicked fingers probed every crevice, and his thigh slowly ground circles into my groin.

Then he was gone.

I fell to the ground, empty and alone.

I awoke, gasping for air. What time was it? What day was it? A dreadful sense of foreboding swept over me.

Burn placed a soothing hand on my arm. "Edward?"

"Something terrible is going to happen."

"What is it?"

I shook my head.

"Edward?"

"I didn't see any details; I only felt. Something is going to happen to you. Soon."

Burn ran his hand up and along my shoulder. "It was only a dream," he said, but his face betrayed more.

"You know what's coming for you don't you?"

"Maybe."

"Burn?"

He sighed. "Yes."

"What?"

"I cannot say."

"Why?"

"It is not my place to do so."

I twisted away from him. "Are you planting dreams in my head?"

"No, Edward. I am not."

"So why do my dreams always contain my stripped body and your wandering hands?"

"Wishful thinking?"

Chapter Thirteen

"I'm going back," I said through a mouthful of dry biscuit and gritty coffee.

"Back where?"

"To the ring, or handle, or whatever."

"No. You are not."

"Burn, you can't tell me what to do." I'd read the *Famous Five* books when I was a kid and always wanted my own adventure. Not the huddled on a raft with an annoying native kind; the secret doorway, pirates' treasure, and mystery runes kind.

"It is too dangerous."

"Aren't you curious?"

"Not in the slightest."

"If it's a handle, what does it open? Will we find answers to rid the planet of the Bad Thing?"

"Edward, I –"

"There's a good chance it'll attack my father, again. If I can stop it –"

Burn sighed. "The *Queen* cannot travel up river and it is a fair walk back to the Basin."

"The exercise will do me good."

He sagged. "You do not know what you are doing."

"Are you coming?"

"No."

I shrugged, hopped on to the riverbank, took a deep breath, and marched towards the Basin. Butterflies flittered in my stomach. I didn't have to do this. We could push on to the Landing Plains and I could say goodbye to this weird planet once and for all. But, something was driving me back. Curiosity? Bravery? Or stupidity? I went with the latter.

"Edward, wait."

I knew he wouldn't leave me to the unknown. Burn stepped beside me with an unfinished biscuit in his hand.

"For later?"

He shoved it into his mouth all at once and beamed a crumby grin. I smiled and gave him a friendly push. I was glad of the company.

Shale-filled shallows replaced the bank, then knee-deep water. Burn glanced at the water, the Basin and me, repeatedly.

"Stop it."

"What?"

"The nervous twitch. I wish you'd stayed on the raft."

He stuck out his bottom lip and glared at me. "Looking for the handle is not a good idea."

"Then turn back."

He rolled a low note in his throat and waded ahead of me.

In thigh-deep water, we entered the Basin. An eerie silence hung heavily. The vines blew in the breeze, but made no noise. Burn stopped dead and wrapped his arms around his thin body.

I squinted at the riverbed. "It's not far from here." Burn didn't answer as I took his arm. "What's the worst that can happen?"

"Your death?"

"My death? Not yours?"

He looked away. I strode off, pulling Burn and driving a wave before us.

In the near distance where the river bent, circular ripples spread out across the surface of the water. I crept up on them and peered through the centre. The ring was there, vibrating.

"I've found it."

Burn pulled away so fast that he tripped and went under. I went back and hauled him up. He stood hunched, like a drowned bronze weasel, scowling at me. "Edward, nothing good will come of this."

"Is that your *spidey sense* again?"

"I am serious." The cheery charmer had disappeared and a frightened boy stood in his place.

"I know you are," I said soothingly. "Can you hear anything in your head?"

Burn's eyes glazed over for a moment. "There is a faint chatter."

"No words?"

"No."

I reached down, grasped the ring with both hands, and twisted. It didn't budge. I nodded to Burn. "Do you think you could help?"

"No."

"Burn!"

He rolled his neck and gave me a dismissive look before he also took hold of the ring.

"One – No, not yet!"

Burn twisted. With my eyes shut and teeth clenched, I twisted. And again. It turned. A grating noise split the silence.

"What the fuck was that?" I spun my head around in time to see a rocky door reveal itself in the far wall of the Basin. Clouds of grey dust wafted up as an entrance about the height and width of a dwarf gaped behind the vines.

"What is that?" Burn asked.

"The back door to Erebor."

"What? It is not funny."

"Nothing. Lighten up."

"There could be anything in there."

"Like what?"

"Dragons."

"Dragons wouldn't have a door that needed a hidden handle." I gripped his shoulders and pointed him towards the secret door.

We picked our way across the barren land between the river and the door. We carefully avoided a copious amount of spiky eight-legged insects and stood in front of the entrance. The smell of decay was overpowering, and heat radiated from inside the black hole. I ducked, took a single step in, and peered into the gloom. "Hello?" The word bounced off the walls and disappeared into – God knows.

"Edward, do not attract attention."

"Come on."

"What! Without a lamp?"

"Yes, Burn, without a lamp." The dirt floor of the tunnel sloped down and the ceiling glowed, like a thousand blue-green glow-worms running on half power. There was enough light to see and, as I made my way down a rock tunnel, my heart beat with excitement, not fear. I glanced at Burn's bottom half silhouetted in the doorway. "Are you coming?"

He bent so his face appeared at the opening. "Are you mad? You have no idea what is in there."

"Burn, live a little."

"My life is fine, thank you."

"Are you sure?"

A moment passed before there was a rush of air as he sped to my side and tutted. "I think I preferred the sulky, silent Edward. He would not have walked down a scary tunnel."

"I thought you'd prefer the more manly me?" I flexed my arms in a mock strong man pose. "I am brave and fearless and – virile," I said in a low voice.

Burn flushed but didn't reply.

I was expecting the bone-numbing cold that you experience in deep caves, but the air was warm. The whiff of rot had faded, or I had got used to it.

Burn balled his fist in my T-shirt and towed along behind me. Without looking, I could see the pouting mouth and screwed up eyebrows.

"You can wait for me outside."

"No. You will need me before the day is out."

"What do you know?"

"It is a sensation more than knowledge."

I spun round, but with his fist still bunched in the back of my shirt, I ended up wrapped in his arms. He appeared ghostly in the spooky light. "What is it?" I asked.

"Something ancient – and primal."

"Look, I'll do you a deal; if we walk for another half hour and see nothing, we can leave."

"Okay."

I made to de-tangle myself from his arms but he hung on. "And play the truth or challenge game," Burn said.

"What?"

"And play the truth or challenge game," he repeated, with wide eyes and the tip of his tongue sticking out the corner of his mouth.

"You really are nuts. Okay, okay."

The glow from the ceiling spread on to the walls and edged the floor. The increased light allowed us to move faster. Burn paced out in front of me, the promise of leaving the tunnel and playing his stupid game spurring him on. I'm guessing it involved nakedness. He needed to see a doctor; his hormones were out of control. And mine seemed to have also come out to play.

For most of the time, the tunnel had been straight and on a shallow downwards angle. Now, the ceiling rose, the walls curved, and the slope became so violent that I considered sitting on my arse and sliding the rest of the way. A tortuous drip, drip, drip, of unseen water blended with a fresh rotting smell to turn my stomach.

A chatter in our heads made us both skid to a halt. Words but not words echoed around my skull.

"What the *fuck*?" I whispered.

Burn shrugged.

"I have a funny feeling someone knows we're here."

We crept around a bend, me in front with Burn breathing hard on my neck behind. The corridor widened and to one side there was a small cavern. It was the only feature I'd seen since we'd first stepped over the threshold. Relieved to break the suffocating monotony, I edged in. A square hole in the far wall glimmered with a yellowish-brown light.

A sudden intense musk smell filled my nostrils, causing me to cough – and an all-consuming desire coursed through me at the speed of light. Beyond my control, my body reacted. The impulse to take Burn there and then was intense. Groaning with the overpowering urge, I pulled him into my space, and wound my fingers through his hair. I yanked his head back, exposed his throat, and sucked welts in a feverish vampire attack before moving on to fresh skin. He cried out. With desire or pain? I didn't care; the impulse to ravish him was stronger. Then, the hunger disappeared as fast as it had arrived.

My shoulders slumped and my head dropped to my chest. I stepped away, but not before stroking my fingers along Burn's cheekbones. "I'm sorry. I don't know what came over me." A hot rush raced up my body and coloured my cheeks.

Burn rubbed his bruised neck. "Do not apologise. My pleasure," he croaked.

I smoothed my clothes before pulling Burn towards the hole. "Maybe the answer to the sudden – need – is in here?"

We peered through – then lurched away. I lowered my voice. "What the *hell* are they?"

"I have never seen their like before."

We both inched back towards the window and stared at the most amazing thing I'd ever seen. Before us stretched a vast cavern with a high vaulted ceiling and rough-hewn walls with its end fading into darkness. Row upon row upon row of raised boxes containing soil and little brown dots, which I presumed to be fungi, ran the length of the room. The cavern was silent apart from an annoying hum, like a fridge on the blink. Tending to the crop were hundreds of – people.

They weren't people, but I had no other word for the humanoid-shaped creatures. They were translucent, like jellyfish, with over-long arms and pulsing internal organs, and every bone in their tall, thin frames was visible. Their bodies emitted a glow, the same as the walls in the tunnel. And they were all moving and shifting around each other, so when they bunched up, it was difficult to spot individuals as their see-through bodies merged into one. They were mesmerising, exotic and alien – proper alien, not like Burn and Naylor. I shuddered. I'd seen these creatures before, in the dream I'd had before we'd set off on my journey home. What the hell did it all mean?

Burn twisted the hem of his shirt around his fingers. "I have never seen or heard of such creatures. What do you think they are?"

"Morlocks."

"What? Edward, why do you speak in riddles?"

I shook my head. "What's the plan?"

"The plan is we leave."

"Leave? I want a closer look."

"Something awful will happen, I can feel it."

"But it's aliens, Burn, real aliens. There would be people on Earth who would kill for the opportunity to meet and study them. My father included."

Burn poked me in the side. "I *am* a real alien."

"You're not. And correct me if I'm wrong, but *you're* obsessed with an alien and his life."

"Who?"

"Me, you idiot."

He blushed as an eerie blue-green glimmer lit the room. Turning slowly from the window we saw a group of glowing Jelly people standing in the entrance. And behind them hovered The Bad Thing. On a leash.

A sudden cold struck my core and my breath hitched. What the *fuck*? We're dead. I scanned the small chamber. There was no escape, unless we leapt out of the two-storey window. Then a random thought – how have they tethered a cloud? I glanced at Burn. He was unmoving, with a wide-eyed gaze flicking from The Bad Thing to the Jelly people, and back again. Close up, their facial features had become clear. Two almond-shaped holes sat between two unblinking jet-black eyes, and a fine line, as if someone had drawn it with a blue pen, indicated a mouth.

You have saved the Collector a job.

Great, more fucking telepaths. "The Collector?"

The alien at the front of the group yanked the leash, forcing The Bad Thing to bob on the end like a docile pet.

Its orders were to retrieve the aliens.

"You're the alien, mate."

Unfortunately, it developed a taste for you. And I do not blame it.

If it had eyelids, I'm sure at that point it would have winked. Burn stifled a nervous giggle. I stamped on his foot. He shot me a look.

As an attempt at inter-species diplomacy I asked, "What is your name?"

We have no name, but the surface people refer to us as the Ancients and your friend calls us the Bloom. Its eyes browsed Burn's body as he staggered back a few steps and paled even more.

"What's wrong, Burn?"

"Nothing." He stood tall and smoothed down his shirt.

"You know them, don't you?"

"Yes, if they are the same Ancients the storytellers speak of."

"So why did you call them the Bloom?"

He shrugged. "It is the name for a group of jellyfish." So much for bloody diplomacy. Burn positioned himself in front of me and cleared his throat. "What do you want with us?"

From you? Nothing. You have done your job.

What did that mean?

From Edward – everything.

They knew my name. Of course they did. Nothing was private on this planet. It exposed my thoughts, my feelings, and my desires, for all to share.

Stepping beside Burn, I said, "What do they mean, you've done your job?"

"I have no idea."

I scowled at him.

"Edward, I swear I do not know what they are talking about."

Enough, the time has come.

A spindly arm reached for me. Long fingers connected with my forehead and hot waves pulsed down my neck and into my chest. My body stiffened. Burn screamed.

Black and white images flashed across my vision – my childhood, my parents, my friends and Burn. The images changed into computers, telephones, and television. Pictures of babies, people having sex, and phallic objects, followed. They moved so fast they blurred into one another.

I passed out.

And opened my eyes to a blur of grey. Tremors quaked through my body and my head throbbed. Where the fuck was I? My fingers felt a hard edge running parallel to my side. I walked them up and over my head and blinked to clear my vision. What the *hell*? I was lying flat in a see-through box. Criss-crossing the lid were ten or so wires with round connectors that pulsed with light.

I banged my fists against the lid and shouted. No reply. Pulling my sleeve over the heel of my hand, I spat on it and cleaned a window in the grotty glass. There was nothing above me but a rocky ceiling. And all was quiet, apart from my heart beating in my ears and the rag of my breath. What did they want with me? Where was Burn? Had he succumbed to the same fate? I cleared a hole to my side and peered through expecting to see another box with Burn's cheery face staring back at me. There were just shadows. I took a deep breath, and then another. At least I was alive. For now.

Someone had to come for me soon. Didn't they? Surely, I wouldn't be left here in this coffin – or life support, or whatever it was. Enclosed spaces had long been a terror of mine since I got stuck in an overcrowded tiny lift full of drunken party people. As time ticked by, I fought to control my breathing.

A loud *tap tap tap* on the box lid made me jump and I swore in surprise. My swearing was way out of control these days.

"Edward."

"Burn, thank God."

His freckly face peered through the clearing in the muck. He grinned at me – for far too long.

"Burn!"

"Yes."

"Stop staring at me and do something."

"Oh, yes." Fingernails scraped along the edge of the box for one teeth-jangling moment as Burn muttered under his breath.

"It is jammed or glued."

"Great."

"Cover your face."

"What!"

"Just do it."

"Burn, don't smash it. *Don't*. Burn!"

Too late. In the tiny window, two hands wielded a large rock. I twisted my head to the side, covered it with my arms, and prayed to God that his aim was good.

The lid smashed, shards rained around my shoulders and head, and the rock landed on my chest with a sickening thwack. Stars burst behind my eyelids and nausea enfolded me. I cried out.

Burn pulled me up from the wrecked box and yanked me behind a rocky outcrop. I wilted to the floor; Burn sat cross-legged with his knee in my lap. Shaking glass from my hair, I risked a glance into the chamber. It was small and had the same blue-green glow. The lack of natural light was making my eyes sore and giving me a headache.

The smashed glass box was a central feature in the room with wooden containers, woven sacks, and rolled up animal skins stacked around it. I guessed it was a store room and I'd been left there until they decided what to do with me.

The glass splinters had left little stabs of pain on any exposed skin. I stroked my face and my fingers came away wet with blood.

"Thanks, Burn, you've scarred me for life."

"But you are free."

"Yes, but scarred for life," I repeated.

"You look – rugged."

"I'm guessing you like that."

"I have a liking for rugged types."

"Burn, you have a liking for any type."

"Edward, that hurts."

"Good."

We sat in silence for a moment.

"That was your worst idea to date."

"Free. That is all I am saying." Burn crossed his arms, and in the eerie light, his face creased into a scowl.

I sighed. "What happened?"

"They zapped you but let me go."

"Why?"

"I have no idea but I ran away from them, down the tunnel, and hid to watch where they took you. They carried you to this room but closed the door so I could not see what was happening. I waited in the shadows until they came out – which was a pointless exercise as they were aware of my presence."

"How?"

"Because I knew that they knew."

"Eh?"

"The point is, why did they let me hang around? It was obvious that

I would try to free you."

"They didn't bargain on you launching a rock at me."

"Probably. In my head, I could hear their conversation. They said they wanted to integrate you."

"I'm sorry. Integrate me? Into what?"

"The hive mind."

"The hive mind. Fucking hell, it's the Borg Collective."

"Edward, your constant references to things I do not understand is infuriating."

"Welcome to my world of the annoying companion. I find it comforting. Anyway, what does that mean for me?"

"I only got parts of the conversation as they used some words I did not understand. But it seems they are unhappy because you are upsetting the delicate balance of our planet with your machines and alien ways."

For the first time in a long time, I was speechless. I was just an Earth boy with an explorer father: how could I upset a whole planet?

"And it seems their society is motivated by sex," Burn continued.

I heard that word. "Sex?"

"Yes. To reproduce is the driving force behind their culture." He paused. "I also got the impression that males and females of the species all did it with one another."

"You'd fit right in, then."

"It does sound fun."

"Maybe – their heightened desire filters through to the surface somehow. Or is passed on by telepathy?"

Burn stared at me with surprise on his half-lit face, and spoke slowly. "When did you get so clever?"

"Thanks."

"It is a possibility – though I would not wish it that way."

"So why do they want me?"

"Hormones."

I made a circular motion with my fingers. "Expand."

"Your raging hormones are perfect fuel for their fire. So to speak."

"Before I started this trip, my hormones were not *raging*."

"Are you sure?"

"Yes."

He grinned. "It is me, then, that lights your fire."

"I'm not sure about that, but something has changed. Do you think these creatures have affected me?"

"Possibly, but I would like to think it is me."

I shoved him, and he puffed up a red dust cloud as he slapped the floor. "Ow. Was that necessary?"

"Yes. It satisfied me." I pointed a finger at him. "And don't say *you* can do that." My stomach gurgled. Burn's dry biscuits and honey suddenly appealed. "Let's go."

"That is easier said than done."

"Why doesn't that surprise me?" I hauled myself out of the dirt and held my hand out to Burn. He took it and we stood for a moment, fingers entwined. How had I ended up under the crust of alien planet, trapped by Jelly people, scarred, filthy, and holding hands with a native boy? Maybe I would write the story one day and call it *The Copper River*. No, that was a crap idea. I pulled him away from the eerie chamber and headed towards the door.

"They will know you have escaped the box."

I opened the door a crack and peeked through. Nobody there. Why? Were we the prey in a sick game of kiss chase?

We tiptoed into a tunnel that looked the same as the first. A little way down it forked into two, and then one of those forks divided into three. "Where are we?"

"In one of the tunnels."

"I know that, you idiot. Are we near the exit tunnel?"

"Oh, I do not know. They all look the same."

"When you followed them, was it for a long time?"

"Relatively."

"What does that mean?"

"I was concentrating on you, not on where they were going."

"Okay. Let's take the right hand tunnel. I heard you always take a right turn to get out of a maze."

"On Abaytor, we say to turn left."

"Of course you do."

We crept along the walls and took the right fork. The heat in the corridor increased, along with the rot smell. Why were telepathic creatures letting us sneak away? I slammed to a halt. Burn bumped into my back. Taking the scruff of his neck, I tugged him round to my front.

"The Bad Thing." We spoke as one.

"Or the Collector. They don't want to get their delicate hands dirty chasing after us. Why should they, when they can send their pet instead?"

Burn's eyes bulged.

"Don't worry; it's me it's got a taste for."

"I can understand that."

I couldn't pinpoint when I liked Burn. He'd crept up on me unannounced, got under my skin and worked his way into my affections. And I was okay with that. I draped an arm around his shoulder. "Come on."

"The pungent air tells me we are nearing the farm." Burn overtook me and peered into the gloom.

"That's the wrong direction. We need to head away from it."

"I would like to see their farming methods. How are they growing crops underground? Do they have animals?"

"Burn, I don't care." I spun on my heels. "Let's go back."

"Please, Edward, I might learn something I could tell my tribe."

Abaytor was way behind Earth; of course Burn wanted to learn any new methods he could. I sighed. "On your head if we are caught."

"Capture is inevitable. We are the mouse that a cat plays with before eating it."

"Nice analogy."

The corridor widened and sloped towards an arched entranceway. To one side was a narrow fall-back with a good view through into the huge farming chamber. We squashed into its shadowy recess. The walls were wet with moisture and green with algae. As we squatted on to the floor, my clothing rucked and dampened. A swampy stink rose around me. "Well, you were totally wrong about the waterfall cleansing spell."

"Yes, but it was fun."

I slapped his shoulder.

From this distance, it was clear the raised beds held fungi. It was watering time, and a fine mist sprayed from holes in a hose strung above the soil. Every row contained spores in different stages of growth. Some beds were empty, and some were yellow-brown with shrivelled capped mushrooms. A few Bloom tended to the crop. My head was buzzing with questions, worries, and fears; I presumed Burn's was also. It was curious that they didn't once glance in our direction.

Burn placed a hand on my arm. "Look into the shadows at the back of the room."

I squinted into the gloom. Nearer, it was possible to see a huge grey organism, the size of a blue whale, quivering in the dark. Millions of shoestring-sized fibres snaked away from it and into the rows of beds.

"That's the daddy."

"I think you will find it is the mother and the fungi are her babies."

I shuddered. "Have you got what you need? Can we go?"

"Yes. We tried growing fungi on open plains, exposed to the sun, thinking that every plant needed sunlight. We were wrong. I can now tell my people to grow it underground with spray watering. We will have another crop to feed our animals and us. This is valuable knowledge, Edward."

"I understand." For me, choosing between shrink-wrapped chestnut mushrooms or expensive oyster mushrooms was my only dilemma.

A smell of musk mixed in with the swamp stink and a wave of nausea swept over me. The Bloom stopped, laid their tools on the beds, and a hum vibrated around the inside of my skull. They slid towards their closest companion and performed an odd gyrating dance, grinding their bodies together while their spindly arms moved in a caressing blur. There were threesomes, foursomes, and even the odd one 'going it alone'. The most erotic noise I'd ever heard purred in my head. I shuffled to one side so Burn couldn't see my body's reaction. A pointless move: he knew what the gyrating bodies and the sensual sound were doing to me, because he was also struggling with his urges. Where I had shifted away, he nudged towards me.

He coughed to clear his throat. "Edward."

"Don't speak. I'm trying to control it," I puffed.

"Why? Let it happen."

I didn't know what day it was but I knew I didn't do guys. Did I? I could do Burn, just him, not boys, just Burn. That would be okay. Wouldn't it? I'm leaving Abaytor. Who would he tell? I knocked my head against the wet wall a few times before slipping my hand around his neck and pulling his face to mine. With his mouth parted and his eyes wide, he wound his fingers in and out of the hem of my shirt – waiting for the nod to remove it. We breathed each other's air for a long moment.

"Is this stinking hole the best place?"

Burn grinned. "I don't care where. It is the fact you have not dismissed me that fills me with joy."

For all that's holy, he's right; I'd weighed up the possibilities and concluded that it would be okay. Then, as if someone had hurled a bucket of ice water over me, the desire disappeared with a shudder. I glanced towards the Bloom; they had resumed their duties. "I'm sorry." I wish I'd never come to this bloody planet. There, I was Edward, a guy with a different girl every night, who liked to party and had no worries or responsibilities. Here, my hormones were out of control, I had feelings for a wayward boy and was in constant fear for my life.

I shifted away.

Burn remained in the same position. "I am going to need some private time – soon."

I laughed. "You are understanding of – the confusion."

"When you are not confused, this is how I imagine it to be."

"Burn! Your imaginings are in my head! You're a depraved soul!"

"Thank you."

I dragged him up; we slipped out of our hiding place and straight into the path of the Collector.

"I knew it'd come for me." I thrust out my chest and stood straighter. "Come on, then, big boy."

"No!" Burn snatched my arm and hauled me away.

"Burn, we can't run from it."

"We can try."

"And run forever?"

"You are leaving Abaytor, it will not be forever."

"It will go after my father, his team, and anyone else who visits the planet. It needs to be stopped." I pulled away from his grip.

The Collector filled the tunnel with its dense broiling mass – waiting. It knew I had no choice.

I took a deep breath and glanced at Burn. "Find me."

"I will." Dirt lined his pale face and the white of his eyes reflected the blue-green glow.

I stepped towards the Collector as smoky tendrils reached out. Burn shouted as it sucked me in. Suspended in its depths, I was frozen and spinning. It glided away from the farm. This time there was no pain, no life-suck. But I drifted in and out of consciousness, until dreams mixed with reality.

A voice in my head said, *Drop*. Drop? The Collector *was* a dog. I fell out of the beast's innards like twisting down a helter-skelter and smacked the earth. "Ow." Hands were on me, running across my chest, feeling my forehead and forcing my eyelids open.

"*Fuck* off." I thrashed my arms and legs wildly.

"Edward, Edward, it's me, it's your father."

Shaking my head, I focused on the blurry outline. "Father?"

"Yes."

"Where is it?" I twisted around looking for the Collector.

"It slithered out." His worried eyes stared back at me. "What happened to your face?"

"It's a long story." I scrambled to my feet feeling okay considering I'd been in the Bad Thing's belly. "What are you doing here?"

"I was collected." He glanced over his shoulder. "Have you seen them?" he whispered.

"Yes, up close and personal."

"They're *real* aliens, son. Not like Naylor and his kind."

"My words exactly."

"I asked them how long they'd had been on Abaytor and if they know about Earth. They ignored me. Then –" He stopped and stared at me. "How did you get here?"

I looked at my feet.

"You turned the ring didn't you?"

"Maybe." I kicked the dirt creating puffs of red that cloaked my ankles, and glanced around.

One side of the large chamber contained two glass boxes like the one Burn had smashed, but these were upright and clean. Hanging ominously inside were headsets with loads of wires protruding from them. The opposite wall held a large archway that led into darkness. Cables running from a round console in the centre of the room hooked on to the pulsing connectors on the box lids. My father and I were alone.

"How long have you been here?"

"I'm not sure, a day maybe?"

"Who are they and what do they want?" I don't know why I whispered, as they could hear every thought.

"From listening into snippets of conversation and knowing Naylor's beliefs, I think they are superior beings who somehow, unknown to them, control the surface people –" my father pointed to the ceiling "– so that they live a kind of symbiotic life with their vast decomposing tunnel networks enriching the plant life, which feeds the animals, which in turn feeds the humans."

"How do they control them?"

"Remote influencing is my best guess. I think their gods and myths have been planted to keep them terrified of the unknown, unwilling to ask questions."

"Why do the Bloom want to control them?"

"Why does any group want to control another? Fear? Power? Wealth? Maybe they know about the human tendency for war and they enslave their weaker minds to prevent attack."

I frowned. "Hang on a minute. You have telepathy?"

"It seems I do down here."

"First I've heard about it. Now we're all one big happy family! Talking about family, where's Naylor?"

"If he has any sense, he's making his way back to the Fire Glade and informing the team of my capture."

I wandered over to the console and ran my fingers over the rows of switches and banks of buttons. "So why do they want us? Burn said something about hormones."

"I don't know anything about hormones, but I think those boxes are some form of life support and the headsets plug into our knowledge, feelings, and emotions."

Like Burn did to me, I stepped into my father's space. I was taller by a hand's width, broader and sturdier. I wasn't sure when that had happened. "We have to go."

"Where? That cloud thing will collect us before we get half way out."

"We have to try."

"When did you become so commanding?"

"At some point between the Fire Glade and the Basin."

My father clapped my back then glanced round. "Where's Burn?"

"He's here. Somewhere."

"I don't fancy being mind-fodder today. Let's get the hell out of here."

Light spread across the room. Two Jelly people stood under the arch. Anger fizzed around them, it was tangible in the air, and I could taste it on my tongue. Light pulsed through their bodies like an electrical storm. The cat was bored with the mouse.

My father placed his body in front of mine and gathered me behind his back. "What do you want with us?"

My name is Zaatar and I am the commander. The honour of your integration is mine and the time has come.

"For what?"

The worms.

"Worms?" I moved around to the front of my father.

They will be your new constant companions and I have looked forward to this moment since your ship landed.

"If it's that exciting, why have you waited?" I sneered.

We are hundreds of years old. Waiting for you to come to us is but a mere moment. Zaatar waved a spindly arm. *Enough talk. Take them.*

Two Bloom soldiers, in a blur of transparent bodies, connected their fingers to our shoulders. I gripped the console for support as a copper taste filled my mouth and a river of pain coursed through my body. Time slowed as my legs stood by themselves and my arms crossed my stomach. I had no control over my body as the alien puppeteer forced me to walk towards the arch. Before my father was marched off in front of me, I saw fear lining his face.

Tottering like a string puppet and with an awareness that I may pass out, I left the chamber and headed further into the belly of the Bloom's den.

"I demand to know where you are taking us," my father bellowed.

Soon you will know all.

"Release the boy. Take me. I have the knowledge you require."

Maybe, but you do not have the delicious raging hormones. If Zaatar had a tongue, I'm sure he'd have licked his lips – if, in fact, he had any lips.

We passed chamber after chamber containing glass coffins. All the boxes held a Jelly man or woman; it was hard to tell. These Bloom weren't the same as the others – they had no glow, no pulse of life. Even their black eyes looked blank. I struggled against my captor but it was useless, I couldn't get my paralysed body to respond.

We passed a similar room but this time, the box did not contain a Bloom. It held a creature that even my weird dreams couldn't have conjured up. Its swollen body was an insipid green colour and, in a distorted face, a grotesque mouth sat wonky with yellow teeth protruding at different angles. Under snow-white matted hair, two drooping eyes with half closed lids pleaded for release. "What in God's name is that?"

He is the only survivor from the race that preceded us.

"Don't tell me, you killed them all."

They did not suit our requirements. As inferior life forms, they were useful for hard labour. Apart from him. He used to be their king, and we feed off his anger.

A vile taste in my mouth made my stomach heave. "You're fucking pond life," I yelled. "Who are you to say who lives and dies?"

We are superior.

"You think because they're not the same, you're better?"

Did you not think the same a short time ago?

Oh God, he was right. My cheeks flushed. I believed myself to be better than Burn. Referring to the captive creature, I demanded, "How long has he been here?"

Many life cycles. Enough. Your species talks too much. He drove me further down the corridor and into the shadows. I fantasised about releasing the beast and watching as he took his revenge on the Bloom.

The last chamber on the right had just enough light to see the decomposing bodies of six humans in white boiler suits, hanging grotesquely in their glass coffins.

"What the fuck?" I muttered to my father.

"My guess is they're the remains of Ranger One's crew. I'd heard rumours some government or other had sent a mission to Abaytor but I never knew what happened to them. Now I do." My father wrenched his eyes away.

"I didn't know there were other crews on Abaytor. Why were they sent?"

"They're part of the race for the bees, Edward. The first country to bring back Abaytor's life-saving bees will have the all the glory, money and power." He looked me in the eye and his face showed the years of strain. "But Abaytor is *my* planet. They're *my* bees. It's *my* job."

"Are you doing it for the glory, Father?"

He dropped his head on to his chest and sighed. "No, Edward. That's not what motivates me."

As we were guided past the stomach-churning sight, my father murmured, "God have mercy on their souls."

Dark, damp, and smelling like rain on a hot day, the worm room was the one chamber without the eerie glow. I yearned for fresh air and sunlight. Raised wooden beds clung to the edge, like the ones housing the fungi. The Jelly man's fingers guided me towards the far end of the room. I glanced into the boxes as we passed and wished I hadn't. A sickening mass of glistening worms writhed against each other. These were not common garden worms. They had protrusions, like tiny fingers, wiggling from flared heads that thrashed about as if smelling the air. On a shelf above them, little clear bottles waited in neat rows. Inside each, tiny worms left slime trails across the glass. I sensed they spelt my end. My guide stopped me in front of them.

Zaatar appeared by my side. I lurched with surprise. *These are harvester worms. They connect to your brain stem and transmit information, and then they induce a sleep full of pain.*

My head yelled at my body to move. It wouldn't respond. I glanced at my father; he had his arms clamped by his side, and his head tilted back with his mouth open as if silently screaming. Sweat ran into my eyes, and my throat tightened. "Father. Father? We will not die in this godforsaken hole. Father?" I feared for him more than I feared for myself.

Zaatar wound thin fingers around a bottle and with care, lifted it off the shelf. He held a palm over the cap and it sprang off. *Prepare him.*

A hand forced my head on to my chest. My whole body quaked. With my heart pounding in my ears, I gasped for air and streamed a long string of expletives. Where was Burn? The worm burrowed into the back of my neck and my world ceased to be bearable and became agony. I passed out.

And came to in a glass coffin. Through the lid, I saw my mother, in her Sunday best, smiling at me. In her hands, she held her expensive handbag, the one she took great delight in showing off to her friends.

"Mother?" I mouthed.

She toppled, her head bounced as she whacked the dirt floor, and the bag tumbled from her hands. Bright red blood stained her pale lemon dress. I screamed. She vanished. My father stood in her place. He was young, bright eyed and smiling. In his hands, he flapped the blueprints to the *Wave Rider.* "Father?" The smile dropped as his face wrinkled and browned. "Father." He disappeared. I sobbed and hot tears flooded my cheeks and traced the line of my lips.

Burn appeared. "Burn?" He cried as he threw a wreath of orange flowers at his feet and watched them float off across the dirt. "Burn. I need you."

His blank eyes bore into me. "I know," he said just before he vanished.

Sexual conquests followed. The girl from next door appeared; she looked beautiful, smiling at me with her naked bottom white against the red earth. My fuck buddy from university, with wet hair and a tiny towel covering her, dripped on to the floor. Then she was gone and replaced by Jenny, my first love, who stripped off her clothes until she stood bare and goose-bumped in front of me.

Then, my best friend, Jim, winked at me and ran his tongue across his lower lip. Burn would have a field day if he knew about him. Maybe, in the open brain policy on this planet, he now did.

As these final images played out, my body vibrated and the wires shook. I groaned with the thrill of the pulsing rhythm and the joy filling my thoughts.

I squeezed my eyes shut to bring myself back to the present. "Stop it!" A searing pain shot up my arms and legs as I tried to move. Sucking in long breaths, I fought an overwhelming nausea.

With little head movements, I scanned the box. Two supports held me under the arms; a thick leather band encircled my waist while cuffs fixed my arms and legs into in a star shape, and going by the pressure, a clamp held my head in place. Wires hung all around me like a mass of tangled spaghetti. I guessed they led to the headset and the suckers pinching my face. Tubes also led from the inside of my trousers to the outside of the box, and something coiled around my groin and lower back. I boiled with fury and embarrassment as I fought the urge to throw up.

Time passed. A moment? Two? An hour? I had no idea.

Then the worm wriggled and a lightning bolt of pain flashed into my head and traced my spine. I screamed, stars burst in front of my eyes and the world blurred with tears. I blacked out.

Sucking in a long hard breath, I came to again and tried to relax and ignore the writhing under my skin. Burn will come. He will. I had faith in him. This, however, I'd never tell him.

My father entered my thoughts. "Father?" I twisted my head to the right as far as it would go. I couldn't see anything apart from the side of the box. Same on the left.

We are all feeding off your sexual confusion. The nursery cannot cope with the influx of newlings.

I threw up. Splattering the box and myself.

And your father's knowledge is staggering. We have learnt so much about your backward planet already.

"Let us go, Zaatar," I mumbled.

I cannot. You are too valuable to us.

"And to me," Burn said.

"Burn? Oh, God. Burn." I stared at him through hazy vision.

"I have figured out what you have done." Burn stood near a small round pool hidden in the shadows near the entrance, which I had not noticed before. He looked tired and older than his years.

You should be glad of life.

"I am ashamed. I blame myself."

You have done your job.

"My job was to get Edward to the Landing Plains. Not to you."

That is what you thought. You also did a good job of stirring hidden desires. They are delicious.

Burn glanced at me with his eyes watery. He mouthed, "I am sorry."

"It's not your fault," I croaked.

Burn turned to Zaatar as three of his soldiers moved to his side. "I know you do not control my feelings for Edward. They are real."

We heightened your desire.

"I am not your puppet," he yelled and wiped his eyes.

That is exactly what you are.

What the fuck were they talking about? What had they done to him?

Burn's hand shook as he delved into his small waist bag. "You will not have him, or his father."

The Bloom vibrated. If I didn't know any better I'd say they were laughing.

You are not strong enough to defeat the hive mind.

"Maybe, but I know how bees operate. I am the number one beekeeper in the Fire Glade."

He was the only beekeeper in the Fire Glade.

"And I know how to destroy a hive." Burn held his arm out. In his hand, he clutched two bars of soap. "Bees hate soapy water." He sidestepped towards the blue pool and held his hand over the surface. "These in your water supply will kill your crops and ruin your drinking water. Now, let them go."

That's where he'd been hiding the bloody soap.

And if we do not?

"You know I have nothing to lose. In the time it takes to zap me, I can drop the bars."

The water will soon replenish.

"Yes, but how long will that take? Your crops and your worms, which I am presuming is your meat, how long can they last? Can you risk it?"

Zaatar's face pulsed with light and a long silence followed. Burn never moved. I held my breath.

If we release them, you will not get far; the Collector will come for you.

"That is a risk I am willing to take."

We know you, Burn; you do not have the courage to destroy us.

"You do not know me." He made a false move to drop the soap. The Bloom lurched forwards.

Our lives run parallel with yours. You cannot harm us without harming yourselves.

Burn remained solid. "Let them go."

At this moment, he looked so dashing.

It was quiet, apart from the worms scuffling through the soil. Then, Zaatar flicked his hand and droned a high-pitched noise. My personal neck worm stopped writhing, the nagging pain stopped, and the tension released from my body. I hung from the supports like a wrung out rag. My heart beat in my throat and I had a mammoth headache. The lid opened of its own accord and the wrist and ankle cuffs retracted. With stiff fingers, I undid the waist belt, wrenched off the headset, and crumpled to the ground.

"I want safe passage. I have noted the other supply pools and there is more where these came from." Burn made to drop the soap again.

You will not be gone long. The Collector will bring you back and this time we will not let you live. Zaatar nodded to his minions, and they moved to the far side of the chamber.

I scrabbled to my feet and searched the room for my father. He was hanging from the supports in a box behind mine.

"Father. Father?" I unhooked him from the machine and bore his full weight as he fell on to me.

He may not have survived the process.

My father was strong both physically and mentally. Of course he'd survive. Grabbing the waistband of his jeans, I heaved him into a half-standing position. He groaned. I pulled him through the chamber. As we passed the soap-holding Burn, I leaned over and kissed his forehead – wrong time and place, but I didn't care. Surprise crossed his face before he threw my father's dangling arm over his shoulder. We ran, trailing my father's size tens in the dust as we went.

"I have found another exit. It is small and reached by climbing, but it is close."

"Climbing? My father's heavy."

"One can push and the other can pull."

"Burn, I don't have the strength."

"You have no choice, Edward."

Around a corner, a thin beam of white light cut across rough-hewn steps hacked into the rock. I took my father's arms and Burn shouldered his backside. He moaned as we jostled him towards the narrow fissure that spelt freedom.

"Is he okay?" My father hadn't opened his eyes once.

"He needs rest."

Something in Burn's voice said *liar*. I stopped and slumped on to the steps; my father fell across my lap. "I can't do this, Burn." My head felt wobbly, and I couldn't focus. Burn squeezed beside me and pressed two finger pads on to my father's neck. "He is weak, if we do not get medical help –" he paused "– I do not like his chances."

I heaved him back up and pulled his dead weight up the steps. "What about the worms?" I pressed my spare hand on to the back of my neck and wished I hadn't. It came back bloodied.

"My guess is the link is broken and it will die soon."

"And if it doesn't?"

"I have a sharp knife –"

"Whoa, you're *not* digging around in my neck."

"We will see. Our first priority is your father."

My father wouldn't die. Only people in films die from alien transmitter worms. *We'll get him to the raft, Burn will work some of his herbal magic, and all will be well.* I turned my attention back to my rescuer.

"Burn, what did they mean by you have done your job?"

"It is not important."

"Are you keeping secrets from me?"

"Yes. I am."

"I'll make you tell."

"I can think of many, *many* ways."

Despite our situation, I laughed. "I'm sure you can."

The narrow opening was smaller than it appeared from the bottom of the stairs. We removed my father's coat, breathed in, squeezed through the gap, and emerged at the river's side of the Basin, squinting into the sunlight. A ledge, the width of an arm's stretch, separated the copper water and us. I carefully put my father down. "Now what –"

"Edward." A low moan followed my name.

"Father? I'm here." I knelt beside him.

"You –" He swallowed. "Must not destroy … them." Every word was a struggle. "They are a … symbiotic race – like the bees are to our world, the Bloom are to this one. Burn –" he coughed "– and Naylor cannot survive without them." He said this without opening his eyes or moving his body.

"Don't worry father, you'll be safe soon." I smoothed a hand across his brow before walking over to where Burn poked half out of the fissure. "Plan?"

"Um, to get him to the *Queen*."

"Through the water?"

"Okay. I will go for the raft and pull it back."

"I'm stronger than you, I'll pull it back. You stay with my father." As I prepared to leap into the river, a faint voice said, "Edward. Here. Burn. Over here."

I searched along the bank and spotted the cataraft some distance away. Naylor was leaping around and waving his hands. Thank God.

The familiar hum of engines filled the Basin as Naylor sped towards us.

"You came back," I said as the cataraft pulled up.

"I never left. Seeing the *Queen* moored down river, I sensed you had turned the ring, so I waited. I heard them, the other people. I know what they intended to do to you."

"What they *did* to us. My father needs attention." I made to jump on to the deck but with my eyesight still fuzzy, I misjudged the distance and toppled in. Naylor hauled me to my feet. "Fucking worm. Burn, pass my father." Burn heaved his body on to the bouncy sides as I grasped Father's arms and pulled him in.

"Edward," my father moaned. I fell to his side. "Listen to me. You and your mother … paid a heavy price for my missions and … I bitterly regret that." He took a ragged breath.

"Don't speak, Father, conserve your energy." Picking up his cold hand, I held it to my cheek.

"Abaytor's bees, Edward … without them our world dies … Do you understand, boy?"

"I understand, Father, of course I do." I spoke the words he wanted to hear but I had no fucking idea what he was talking about.

"My mission is secret … the government didn't want widespread panic. It's imperative, Edward, that the bees are exported."

Bees? I didn't understand the fuss surrounding Burn's little buzzy friends. However, I said, "Of course, Father."

"Do you understand, boy?" he repeated.

"I understand," I lied.

He expelled a long and painful breath like a weight had been lifted. "I never wanted any of the fame … I'm just a scientist with an urge to explore but it turned into more … much more."

Shushing him, I pulled a blanket over his chest.

"I was never … a good father, I am … sorry … son. I …" My father's back arched as he coughed. Then he flopped and his head lolled to one side.

"It's okay, Father. Father?"

Naylor dropped to his knees and laid his head on his friend's chest. He held up a finger to ask for silence as he listened for a heartbeat. Then, he grabbed a limp wrist and held it to his face for a long, *long* moment.

Naylor stared into my eyes. I smiled at him. I had no reason to fear.

"He has gone."

Silence.

"Gone where?"

"To be with his God."

"He doesn't believe in God. What are you talking about?" I fell by his side. "Father? Wake up." I tapped his face but something about the way his head wobbled stopped me. "Father?"

Naylor took my arm. "Edward –"

I wrenched away from him. "No. You're wrong. Burn?"

Burn placed a hand on my father's neck and stared into the distance. "Edward. I am sorry." Tears cut lines in the dirt on his face. Why did I notice that?

"No. You're both wrong." I shook him. "Father?" I shook him again. "Father!"

"Edward, I am so sorry, he has gone," Naylor mumbled.

"He hasn't. I have to tell him about my adventures." I took his hand, patted it and whispered, "You can't die. I need you to be proud of me."

Burn gently lifted me into his arms and held me as my knees buckled. I let him take my weight and sobbed into his neck, "We never worked it out."

"I know, Edward. I am so sorry," Burn breathed into my ear.

Through tangled copper hair, I saw Naylor's bow. "I'll kill him." I shoved Burn away and snatched the weapon.

Burn staggered back a few paces. "Who?"

"Zaatar," I spat.

"You will not." Burn lunged for me.

I sidestepped, and he fell on to the deck. "You can't stop me."

"Edward. No." He seized my ankle as I stepped off the cataraft. I tumbled and smacked the rocky ledge with a sickening thud.

"Get the fuck off me, Burn." I booted his hand.

"Ow. Edward, did you not hear your father's final words? He said the Bloom and the surface people are connected."

"So?"

"So? You are not a native of this planet. It is not your place to start a war between our peoples."

A war? I lay on my back sucking in air as if it was in short supply. My neck was sore and, even though the sun shone, I shook with cold. I threw the bow to one side and wept at the suffocating loneliness and loss.

Burn crawled by my side and pressed against me. I took comfort from his body heat. "What now? I can't take him home, the journey is too long."

Naylor scrambled on to the ledge and placed a hand on my arm. "I can take him back to the Fire Glade. He will be buried with honour."

Buried? I didn't know if he wanted burying or cremating or something else. I sat and nodded numbly. How the fuck do I know if I've made the right decision? In the space of ten minutes, I'd stepped up a rung on the ladder of life and become an orphan.

"Will you be coming back with me?" Naylor asked.

"No. I'm going home."

"Are you sure, Edward? You may regret that decision."

"I need to be at home. There's nothing here for me." As I said the last part of the sentence, I winced. "Burn, I didn't mean –"

"It is okay, Edward. I understand." However, his face said otherwise.

The three of us sat huddled on the rocky ledge staring into the bobbing cataraft cradling the body of my father.

"If you are sure, I will prepare for the journey home."

"The rest of my father's team are still in the Fire Glade. He won't be alone." I slid an arm around Naylor's shoulders. "You're a good friend and I won't forget what you have done for us."

"If it means anything, I know he was proud of you."

Tears welled. "If that is true, it does mean a lot. Thank you."

I clambered back into the cataraft, knelt by my father, and arranged his arms across his chest. I bent to kiss his forehead and opened my mouth to speak but no words came, so I pulled a blanket over the top half of his body and climbed back to Burn's side.

"Take care, boys. The Bad Thing is still hunting you."

"We can handle it."

"I am not so sure."

I watched Naylor take my father away. I hoped to God that my mother wasn't looking down and blaming my errant ways for my father's death.

"Oh, God, Burn. Am I doing the right thing? Should I be going back with my father?"

"What is pulling you the strongest at the moment? Your father's burial or home?"

"Home," I said weakly.

He took my arm. "Home it is," he replied, and then telepathically, *"It was not your fault, Edward."*

"Burn, get out of my head."

"You did not send the Collector for your father, the Bloom did."

I studied the black rings around his eyes and his wonky stance.

"I need a drink. Is there any mash on the *Queen?*"

"Yes."

"Fancy getting totally obliterated?"

"Oh, yes."

"I love you, man."

"Of cou-rse you do," Burn slurred back.

I knocked my mash vessel against his. "You're my best friend."

"We both know that is not true, but thank you." Burn giggled and tipped over on to his side.

"Oh, I need to pee." I pushed off the deck and wobbled from foot to foot.

"Shall I come with you?"

"Mate, you can come anywhere with me." I reached out to lift him. He grasped my hand and pulled me over. I ended up sprawled over a honey barrel with my arse in the air and the mash held high.

Burn laughed to excess then sucked in a long breath. "I am going to vomit."

"It's all in the mind. Trust me, I'm a doctor." I toppled off the barrel.

"Are you? Wow!"

"No, you idiot. I'm not. Come on, I really need to pee."

I rolled across the deck but didn't stop at the edge and plopped into the shallows.

"Edward, do not worry, I will save you." Burn's fuzzy face peered over the log deck.

I took his hand and yanked him into the river. He flapped like a fish out of water for a moment then rested his head on my chest.

"Some rescuer!" I shouted. Whoa, that was loud.

"Why are you shouting?"

"Fuck knows."

"Anyway, I have done all the rescuing I intend to do for a long time."

"I never said thank you. Without you, I shudder to think what would have happened."

He smiled and shut his eyes. I shook him. "Burn, wake up."

"I am not sleeping. No. Not me." He shifted his soggy head on to my shoulder and wove his legs through mine. Wet, he was surprisingly heavy. My arms drifted around him. The wooden cup floated from his fingers. "I thought you needed to pee, Ed-ward."

"I did."

"Do not tell me you have done it."

"Okay, I won't."

"Edward, that is disgusting."

"I know." I giggled.

Abaytor's bright moon lit the water lapping at our bodies and stars swam across the alien sky. I searched for Earth. For home.

"I am sorry about your father," Burn mumbled. He knew my thoughts had wandered off.

"So am I, in many ways." I closed my eyes.

"No. Do not sleep. We need to get out of these sopping clothes."

"Also, out of the river would be good."

Burn tumbled off me and crawled on to the bank. "Here. I will help you."

With the planet spinning far too fast, I scrambled next to him and sat on my haunches as Burn shuffled over. He took the top button of my shirt in his fingers and paused. I nodded with more enthusiasm than I expected. Burn undid my shirt and slipped it off my shoulders. A long moment followed where no one moved and no one spoke.

Burn cleared his throat. "Stand."

I duly stood, albeit wobbly.

He ran his fingers along the waistband of my trousers until they settled at the button. He unfastened it and his breathing laboured as he slowly slid the zip open. I shook my hips, and the trousers slipped to the floor. I was naked. I'd given up on undergarments many weeks ago.

Burn staggered off, splashed through the shallows, grabbed a blanket, and held it out. "Here." He spun his head away. "I am not looking."

Something in me screamed, *I want you to look. Look at me. All of me.*

I need your attention. I want your adoration. I want – your hands on me.

Burn groaned. "That is the mash talking, Edward."

I took the blanket. "Maybe."

"What kind of person would take advantage of a drunk who is grieving?"

"Not you?"

"No."

I sighed. "I need to sleep."

Flinging his clothes in all directions, Burn stripped. I noticed with amusement his tunic drifting away. He wrapped one of his favourite Treater blankets around himself and crawled under the canvas. "Are you coming?"

I paused before saying, "Yes." I wriggled in next to him and stretched out.

"You *are* my friend."

"*Best* friend?"

"Let's not go that far."

Burn laughed. "You are buttering me up because you want – um, attention."

"Desperate, actually."

"In the morning, I will remind you that you were so drunk you even considered me."

"I'm *not* drunk."

"You desire sex?"

"Yes."

"With me?"

"Um, there's no one else, so, yes."

"Thanks. You are *very* drunk."

I wished my body would stop tingling. "I need to lose myself, Burn," I pleaded.

"In me?"

"Yes."

"Edward, you are not making it easy. My self-control is not endless."

"Ed."

"What?"

"Call me Ed. All my friends do."

"I cannot change now. You have always been Edward."

"Try."

"Okay, Ed." He swivelled to face me. "No. It is wrong."

"I'm sorry."

"For what?"

"Being a shit."

"Do not apologise. Stop talking. I need to sleep."

"Come here."

"No."

"Please."

Burn snaked over. I lifted my blanket.

Burn sighed. "Edward."

"Get in."

Still curled in his blanket, he pressed into my arms. I craved the closeness of another human being and Burn would do just fine.

On the night my father died on another planet a lifetime away, I slept, with an alien worm in my neck, naked and sloshed, with an equally nude and blotto native boy enfolded in my arms.

The morning brought with it the headache from hell, a too bright sun, a too noisy river, and a sickening awareness of yesterday's events. I sat and swayed for a minute while nausea swept over me. I swallowed it back. Burn had shifted to his side of the tent in the night and I got an eyeful of his pale arse sticking out of the blanket. "Burn." I shoved him. "Burn."

"No. No. No," he groaned. "Do not shout."

"I'm not. Burn."

"What?" He turned to face me and squinted in the light.

"Thank you for not taking advantage of a drunken Earth boy. I owe you one."

"I think you will find you owe me more than one."

The tent darkened as a huge shape blotted out the sun.

Chapter Fourteen

At any other time, streaking unclothed along a riverbank with my family jewels swinging free may have been liberating. But running from the Collector wasn't. Burn, like a naked gazelle, ran a few strides ahead.

"I told you to fill the stove with water, just in case," I puffed.

"You did not tell me anything of the kind," Burn yelled back.

"I did."

"Did not."

"I did."

"Too drunk." He vaulted an exposed tree root.

I did the same. "Was not."

"Wanted sex."

"Oh, I did not."

"Did, too."

"Shut up."

Burn glanced back. "Nice view."

"Not funny. Can you see it?"

"Yes. It moves slowly for an important weapon in the Bloom's armoury."

I looked over my shoulder. The Collector was ten paces behind and shape shifting. It settled on humanoid, planted its feet on the ground, and ran.

"Holy shit." I zoomed past Burn. "It's not moving slow now. It's turned into Usain Bolt."

"Who?"

I grabbed his hand and yanked him to my side. "Faster. You need to run faster."

"This is my highest speed," Burn panted.

The grassy riverbank turned into a thicket of leg-scratching bushes and Burn yelped as I heaved him through. Twisting back, I saw the Collector pumping its smoky arms and legs like the *Terminator* and, just like the mechanical man, it would keep going until we dropped. My knees twanged against something hard – pipe reeds. That was it. I snapped two at the base as we ran past, threw one to Burn, and leapt into the Copper River. Burn sensed my plan and dropped in behind me. Using the reeds as breathing tubes, we submerged ourselves in the cold water. The surface darkened as the Collector hovered above us. I held a finger up to show we wait.

Then, I stopped breathing.

A taste of ash filled my mouth and black dots crowded my vision as I clawed at my throat. I tried to suck air through the pipe but there was none to take. I realised with bile in my throat that I was sucking in the Collector. *No. No. No. I do not die inhaling a fog monster.* Smoke replaced oxygen as my eyes bulged and I clawed for the surface. My mind screamed as my body slowed and stopped thrashing. There was no choice. I gave myself to the inevitable and sank. As the pipe drifted from my mouth and peace washed over me, I saw my father and mother holding hands and smiling.

I opened my eyes a fraction and paused. Filling my vision was a pure white light and silence. Was I dead? Was this heaven?

Then Burn's face appeared in the narrow view and smiled. Was he dead as well? Was I doomed to spend eternity with his grinning face? I opened my eyes fully to see a cloudy sky, and with an enormous effort I shifted up on to my elbows and groaned. "What happened?"

"You owe me one, again."

"Eh?"

"I sucked it out of you."

"What?"

"I hauled you out of the water, clamped my mouth over yours, and sucked out the Collector."

"Just like that?"

"Yes."

"So why aren't you dead or something?"

"I blew it away."

"You blew it away?"

"Yes."

"Where?"

"There." Burn pointed towards an upturned round boat that resembled half a giant walnut floating near the shore. "It is under the quffa."

"So let me get this straight. You sucked the Collector out of me and blew it under the boat?"

"Yes."

"And it can't escape because of the water."

"For now."

"Are you Superman?"

"I do not think so."

"But you are marvellous."

He grinned.

"But why aren't you dead?"

"I do not know." He shifted his position in the dirt.

"Sore throat or anything?"

"No."

I looked down at my body as a cold breeze goose-bumped my bare skin. "So how long have you been sat staring at me?"

"Edward, how could you say such a thing?"

"How long?"

Burn blushed. "Since I knew you were okay."

"You're warped."

"I am not misshapen."

I sensed we were not alone. "Who's there?" I whispered.

"Local fishermen."

"We're naked."

"Yes."

I daren't look round. "What are they doing?"

"Staring."

I swallowed and sat up. Three men and a young boy stood in a line, leaning on sticks with their brown faces blank.

I turned back to Burn. "Now what?"

"Now, we smile." Burn pulled me up. "And walk away."

We didn't walk, we ran.

The *Queen* groaned as she ambled her way down river. She was worse for wear: the tent's canvas roof hung in tatters and now offered little protection, and the logs on her left side parted company regularly. The deck spent an annoying amount of time under the river's surface and most of our belongings were waterlogged.

"I'm not sure she'll make it."

"She has not let us down so far."

"No, but there's still time." The blanket I had slung around my waist slipped down, I hauled it back up and fingered the wet clothes hung from a rope strung across the deck. "These are never gonna dry."

"Be patient, Edward."

"I will carve that on your gravestone."

"What?" Burn blew the dust away from a piece of wood he was whittling like a 1950s Boy Scout.

I shook my head. "What day is it?"

"I do not know."

"How long have we been travelling?"

"Since we set off."

"You are so annoying."

"Still?"

"Yes." I watched him turn and shape the wood. I couldn't figure out what he was carving. It appeared to be a duck but, as he twisted it in his fingers, it resembled a teapot. What I wouldn't give for a decent cup of tea right now. The foul brew that Burn concocted tasted like rusty nails.

"What are you making?"

"It is an offering."

"To who?"

"The god of safe passage."

"You and your bloody gods."

"You may be grateful for one of my gods." He pointed towards a vast empty horizon filled by the haze of the noon sun and nothing else. I shielded my eyes. It appeared as if we were about to float off the edge of the world.

"Burn, this planet is round, so please tell me what *that* is."

"It is an optical phenomenon. Where the light bends through the cold air above into the warm air below, it produces a displaced image of the sky or the earth. The temperature gradient has to be precise –"

"Okay, okay, I get it. So do we sail through?"

"Maybe. But the Ruined Falls are somewhere in this area. They may be just past the false horizon."

"Ruined Falls, they sound – fun."

Burn stood. "We will moor the *Queen* and take a look."

With the raft secured, we trudged through boggy ground towards the haze. The unmistakable roar of furious water struck us as we passed through the shimmer. The serene river had morphed into a violent torrent, tearing a bite out of a lip of the land. Exposed jagged rock protruded into the misty emptiness. The sound was overwhelming.

"I guess this is Ruined Falls?" I yelled as we edged closer and peered into the frothy depths. An angry river charged out of the churning uproar. "Don't tell me, we'll have to carry the *Queen* around."

"No." Burn traced the line of a faint path with his finger. "The route down is short but steep and the raft is too heavy."

My body tensed. "Why is this river the quickest way off this damn planet?" I lifted the blanket and slumped on to the red earth.

Burn sat next to me. "Because the Abaytorian people don't need to be quick."

"Why did you agree to take me home, Burn?" I muttered.

"I have hungered to see beyond the Glade ever since my parents died. Naylor believed I had a desire to flee my grief." He shrugged. "Taking you to the Landing Plains was my opportunity to see other horizons. And spend time with the boy from another world."

I stared at him – dirt smudged his narrow face and his hair was doing a serious impression of a troll doll I had as a kid. "I bet you regret that now?"

He bounced up and dusted his trousers down, not that the action had any effect. "Come on." He reached out a long hand and I took it willingly.

"So run that by me again. We hold on and pray?"

"Yes."

"How about you hold on and I'll walk round."

"Edward, your weight will keep the raft balanced."

"You're going to kill me when we're only a few days from reaching my ship. You realise that'll be the whole Kemp family gone." I flashed a quick smile to cover my pain.

Burn scrubbed a hand across his face and didn't return the smile. "You will not die, Edward."

The shimmering horizon was now close, and black clouds ganged up and threatened to add to our misery. The raft increased her pace as if she were on invisible elastic, drawing us towards the unknown.

"Remember to keep your weight towards the back to keep her from nose diving as we go over the edge."

I shuffled up, sat within the opening of the tent, and forced my fingers into the cracks between the logs. I glanced around; we wouldn't win a Good Housekeeping award. Empty crates and discarded junk littered the *Queen's* deck, and the line of clothing hung limp like wet dishcloths above my head.

"Burn, I've got a funny feeling about this."

"What kind of feeling?"

"It's like I've dreamt this moment."

"All will be well; we have been through much worse."

Famous last words? The raft jolted and reared. "Fucking hell, we're gonna die." The screeching *Queen* rushed toward the frothy lip of land. I hunkered down and held on. As she launched into the air, the crack my fingers were in became a chasm as the two logs separated. For a long moment, there was nothing – time, earth, up or down, just that sensation in your stomach when a car takes a hump-back bridge too fast. Then, the *Copper Queen* smacked the water's surface and I tumbled off, went under, and swirled around in the angry waters like a sock in a washing machine. Sunlight was in view one second and lost the next. I kicked out, pointed my hands towards the surface, and pirouetted like a ballerina in the violent torrent. A long object floated within a body's length, I aimed for it before blackness consumed me.

I came to with my naked skin frozen. Where was I? Where was Burn? The log I was lying on was rough and jutted into my stomach. Was this all that's left of the *Queen*? The black clouds now hung low and growling and torrential rain blurred my vision. The wind-whipped river bucked beneath me. I dug my fingernails in and hung on as the log sailed the high water and with a bone-jarring smack, hit the dips. I lifted my head and adjusted my position, which was a mistake. The log spun and I rolled off into the biting water. Flinging my arms back over it, I hauled myself up. I now lay diagonally, with my arse sticking up.

"Edward!"

Burn. Thank God. I twisted my head, and found him behind me, clinging on to a smaller log, bare-chested, and grinning.

"Nice view. Again."

"Everything is a fucking joke to you, isn't it?" I kicked my legs to steer the log towards an overhanging branch. "I think we've lost the *Queen*."

"We have lost the *Queen*." Burn stroked the log he was riding. "This is the third log from the right."

Grasping the branch, I slid off the log and, hand over hand, pulled myself along until I reached the bank. I was cold, wet, naked, and now homeless. What the hell? Burn copied my monkey moves and dragged himself on to the bank.

"What now?" I asked as a honey barrel floated past.

"We save everything we can." Burn's face was wet. I couldn't tell if it was tears or rain.

I rolled my neck. "I'm sorry. She meant a lot to you."

"More than you know."

She meant a lot to me, too. Like Burn, the ramshackle collection of logs had wiggled into my affections. I hugged him. He was all bony and slippery with rain. Burn froze and his eyes widened. With a sudden awareness of my nudity, I pulled away and patted his back instead.

"Thank you, Edward."

"This is one hell of a trip."

The remains of the canvas tangled in the overhanging branch. Burn stepped into the shallows and pulled it on to the bank. Shielding my eyes against the driving rain, I glanced down river. The broken up *Queen* had snagged behind a group of boulders forming a log dam. Belongings and equipment bobbed in front of it like horses at the start of a race.

"There." I pointed. "Come on." We ran down river lugging the tent behind us and then stood staring at the wrecked raft. Burn slung the canvas over our heads. "I should say a few words."

"Really?"

"Yes."

"Can you make it quick? I'm freezing my nuts off."

"I can help with that."

"Burn!"

He dropped his head to his chest. "You have served me well and will be missed. You were my first raft and I will never forget you, or the times you gave me." He glanced at me. "Your turn."

"My turn?"

"Yes."

I sighed. What do I say? The logs jostled for freedom as the honey barrels bumped against the crates. I took a deep breath. "You did well. Okay?"

Burn threw me a withering look. "One of us has to go in to salvage what we can."

"Not me."

"I did not think so." He waded into the river and sucked in a long breath as the water reached the top of his thighs. "What should I get? We can't carry everything," he said with his voice higher than usual.

"Clothes, skins, food, medicines, and a knife."

"How precise."

My rucksack floated past. "Grab that," I yelled. Burn hurled it on to the bank and I peered at the soggy contents. Music player – no good, I tossed it. Phone – useless, I discarded it. Tablet – ruined, I ran my fingers across the screen and then threw it. Now there was room for food, medicines and clothes.

Burn gathered all we could carry and chucked me a sopping pair of shorts and a T-shirt. I'd forgotten I was naked, again.

"Now what?"

"We can trek the rest of the way in two days."

"How do you know?"

"If you think about it, you know too."

I closed my eyes and concentrated. A map swam across my vision with the Ruined Falls and the Landing Plains clearly marked next to each other. It seemed I had gained built-in Sat Nav.

"We need to find shelter tonight and build a fire. With warm clothes and food in our stomachs, the world will be a happier place." Burn slung the stove bucket across his back, readjusted his bow, and gave his beloved *Queen* one last glance before striding off. My empty stomach felt heavy as I watched the remains of the raft part company with the boulders and zoom off down the river. There was too much loss on Abaytor. I would be glad to get home to my stocked fridge and comfortable bed.

As I followed Burn, I couldn't remember the last time I was dry, warm and still. "My feet are wrinkled, I'm sure my toes are rotting off," I moaned.

"They are not, Edward."

Increasing my pace, I fell in by his side. "My fingers, then." I held out my hand.

Burn took it and studied each finger. "They are fine."

"Your god offering didn't work."

"It seems not."

We walked in silence for a while. "I have to pee."

"Okay." Burn sauntered off.

"Wait for me."

"Wait?"

"Yes."

He sighed. "I will."

I nipped behind a tree. There was something primal and deeply satisfying about peeing outside. I trudged back to Burn's side. "How far till we stop?"

"We can stop whenever you like."

"Now. I want to stop now."

"Edward, are you tired?"

"You sound like my mother."

"Am I right?"

"Yes." I resisted the urge to stick out my bottom lip.

Our first night's camp was under the overhanging bough of an old Dragon Tree. Burn slung the canvas over the lower branches and made a decent tent. He built a fire, steamed our clothes dry, and cooked rice and hard beans called motts.

"So, how long?"

"How long for what, Edward?"

"Till the Collector discovers us again."

Burn glanced skyward. "Not long."

"We have to do something about it."

"You do not have to do anything, you will be home soon."

"I somehow feel responsible."

"Why?"

"The Bloom wanted the aliens, not the natives. If we hadn't come here, you wouldn't have known about them."

"The Bad Thing was still on the loose. I believe the Bloom were also collecting natives."

"You're saying that to make me feel better." I rested my head next to his and enjoyed the heat of the fire and a full tummy. It was the simple pleasures. "I'm sorry about the *Queen*."

"I am sorry about your father. There is no contest, Edward."

"We never got on."

"That does not lessen your loss."

Abaytor's sky was a deep violet and sprayed with stars. I swept my arm across it. "When I was a child I would gaze at the night sky and ask my mother to find my father. Every time I asked her, she would point in a different direction. It didn't matter; to me he was a true star man."

"Did you ever tell him that?"

"No."

"That is a shame."

"Anyway, two more days on this bloody planet, then it's clean clothes and a proper cup of tea."

"Yes," Burn whispered.

"Come with me." The words formed and were out of my mouth before my brain engaged.

168

"Really?"

I faced him. "Yes." Wow. "I mean it. Come with me."

"I am flattered that you have asked but I cannot."

"Why not?"

Burn hesitated before saying, "I would not fit in on your planet."

"I will help you."

He shook his head.

"I thought you'd jump at the chance to explore new horizons and all that."

"Yes, normally I would have loved to but – I cannot."

"Why?"

"You will know soon and I am sorry."

"You're talking in riddles." I scowled at him.

"Edward, run."

"What?"

"*Run.*"

I leapt up and pelted away from camp and into the night. As I ran, I glanced around. Nothing. Being a black cloud in the darkness is good for the Collector but not for me. *Water. I need water.*

Sploshing sounds filled the silence. Burn.

"Edward, where are you?"

"Here."

"Where?"

"How the hell do I know? I'm running past a tree with a hole in the trunk."

"I can see you. Oh, no, Edward, run!" The panic in Burn's voice pumped my legs harder but a familiar chill prickled my skin. As smoky arms embraced me, my heart lurched and the air stole from my lungs. Good God, this thing was really fucking me off now. Should I fight it or give in and hope Burn arrived with water in time? The Collector decided for me as it began to suck out my life force. I collapsed to the ground. The monster squeezed my body, forcing me to gasp for air like a stranded fish.

"Get off him, you Son of a Horeweevil!" Burn yelled as water struck me.

The Collector didn't pull away. Was it becoming used to the water? Shouts filled the air as another deluge struck my crunched up body. It relaxed its grip. "Again, Burn," I cried as another bucketful hit.

The beast released me, morphed into wispy tendrils, and snaked off through the shadowy trees.

Burn hauled me to my feet. "Thought I'd lost you that time."

"I'm bored with this game and the Collector must be getting pretty fed up." I screwed the water out of my T-shirt. "We need a box."

"Box?"

"Like Kai from the Benuim said, we capture it in a metal-lined box so it will blow itself out in fury."

"And how do you intend to do that?"

"I don't. You do."

"Me?"

"Yes. You're the blower."

"My reputation precedes me." He winked.

I scowled at him. "We'll repeat what happened with the pipes and the walnut boat. Except this time it will be the metal box."

"Just like that."

"Yes."

"So where do we get a metal-lined box?"

"Make one or get someone to make one for us. Is there a village near here? Don't answer that." I shut my eyes and searched the mental map. Opening them again, I said, "Yes, it's past the woody thing. There may be a blacksmith, or shoe shodder, or whatever you call them. Maybe they can do something. Why are you looking at me like that?" Burn was staring at me slack-jawed.

"There is something so stimulating when you take control."

"Stimulating?"

"Yes."

"You're weird."

"Good weird?"

I shrugged.

"Ha!" He flung his arms up.

"Don't get too cocky."

"Cocky? Is that good or bad?"

I laughed. "Depends."

"On what?"

"Let's go."

"Now?"

"Yes. We can't stay here now it knows where we are." I took his arm. "Thanks – again."

"Well," he sighed, "I am getting tired of saving your life."

Chapter Fifteen

The blacksmith – muscle-bound, red-nosed and mono-browed – stood with legs apart in front of his forge, smacking an iron rod into the palm of his hand. "You want what?"

"A wooden box lined with metal." I smoothed down a stray bit of hair and hitched up my shorts. "Please."

"Why?"

"It's a trap."

"For?"

"A monster. It doesn't have to be a box. It could be a tube or a triangle or better still, a vessel with a narrow neck. In fact, forget the wood; a metal bottle will be fine."

"A metal bottle?" The man shook his head.

"Yes." I turned to Burn. "We can recreate *Aladdin*."

"What?"

The blacksmith knitted the bar through his fingers. "You boys look like you own the clothes you are stood in and nothing else."

He was right.

"How are you going to pay?"

"Here." I unfastened the strap of my expensive watch. "On my planet, this device is used to move through time. It may need a new battery." Offering it to him, I smiled at his confused face. "It's gold."

"Gold? Okay. Come back in a day." Thick calloused fingers took Switzerland's finest.

"A day!" Burn shoved me. "Right, thanks."

"What do we do for a day? Where do we sleep? What do we eat?"

"Edward, in that time you could be at your ship. You do not have to do this."

"The Bloom murdered my father. If I can't wage war on them, the least I can do is kill their Collector," I snapped.

"It will not bring your father back."

"No, but it'll make me feel better."

"Then I am afraid what I have to say next will make you feel worse."

"What?"

"The shoe shodder's wife has offered us accommodation in return for – um –"

"In return for what? Burn?"

"You tell her all about Earth."

"No. No. No more public speaking."

"She has organised the gathering for after the evening meal."

"Gathering?"

"The village elders, that kind of thing."

"No, Burn."

"Talk or starve, your choice."

"Fucking hell."

The blacksmith's wife was rotund and rosy-cheeked and didn't stop giggling. She ushered us towards a tiny bedroom with one small bed. I glanced at Burn, who grinned back. On the bed were two white nightshirts, clean clothes, and soap. Next to it was a metal bathtub, and next to that a small hearth with a raging fire.

"Nice and cosy," Burn mouthed.

I scowled at him.

A young girl bustled into the room with buckets of hot water and filled the tub. Another followed and did the same.

"Please," the wife said, "clean up, and then come to eat. We are all looking forward to your talk." She swept up the two girls who stood with empty buckets gawping at us and slammed the door behind her.

"Seems your reputation precedes you," Burn said.

"It's not all it's cracked up to be. Do you want the bath first, or me?"

"We could go in together."

I shot him a withering look. "Burn, no. Anyway, it's tiny."

"Ha! You considered it."

"Did not."

"Did, too."

"Shut up and swivel." I made a stirring motion with my fingers.

"What for?"

"So I can get undressed."

"Really?"

He had a point so I sighed and whipped off my clothes. As I lowered myself into the warm water, Burn flopped on to the bed next to me. "Here." He plopped the soap into the bath, watched it sink and settle at my knees.

I chased the slippery bar up my legs and scrubbed my chest and arms. "That was a stroke of genius with the Bloom and the soap."

"Thank you, Edward. I am sorry it was too late for your father."

"Not your fault."

"Not yours, either."

"Thanks." I skittered the soap across the water's surface and slumped into the warmth. My breathing slowed as I closed my eyes.

A figure leaned in. He smelt of the river. I didn't lean away. His hollow eyes searched mine. There was no sound except for my heart clattering in my ears. I took a deep breath and pressed my mouth to warm sweet-tasting lips. He quivered with surprise and emitted a low moan. Insistent hands pressed into my lower back. I drew back. Cold fingers slid down my bare arm and took my hand. "NO!" I shouted. The exclamation surprised me. Then, my hand felt so empty. The figure had gone.

I awoke to Burn studying my face. "The dreams are getting worse are they not?"

"That one was more sensations than images."

"Of what?"

"Loss."

Burn dropped his hand into the bath. "The water is cold."

"Sorry."

"It is okay, I like being filthy."

"Yes, in more ways than one."

The wife marched in with towels. Seeing me in the bath with Burn's arm submerged to the elbow, she dropped the towels on to the bed and carefully made sure she kept her eyes down. She coughed and said, "We are ready when you are," before scuttling out.

Burn threw his head back and guffawed. "Only the gods know what she was thinking."

"I know what she was thinking. Come on, let's get this done."

I leaned against one wall of the room with combed hair, fresh clothes, and a full belly. Candlelight danced shadows on the faces of the gathered villagers. Burn sat at the back with his wild hair tied up, grinning and winking. He's so annoying.

"Why is Nethy making a metal bottle?" a boy at the front asked.

"To catch a catcher."

The boy's eyes widened. "Who?"

"The Bad Thing."

"I heard that thing killed your father." A gruff voice called from the shadows.

I twisted my fingers around each other. "No, it didn't kill my father. Its owners did."

"Who are they?"

I squinted at Burn above the heads of the crowd. He shook his head. "Don't know." My cheeks flushed as I studied the floor. I was never a good liar.

Burn stood. "Tell us about Earth, Edward."

"Yes," voices chorused.

As an ambassador for Earth, I wouldn't have chosen me, but I was the only Earthling in the room, so I told the Abaytorians what I had told the Benuim and answered a hailstorm of questions to the best of my ability.

The bed that night was heaven-sent, even with Burn's elbow in my ribs. "Shift."

"There is nowhere to shift to, Edward."

I twisted on to my side dragging the blankets with me. Burn pulled them back exposing my front to the chilly night air. I sat up. "You lie on your side with your back to the wall and I'll lie on my side with my back to you."

"How lovely."

I snatched the bedding back and flopped on to the pillow. Burn shifted until his body fitted mine. My eyes drooped; I'd grown so at ease with him that I found comfort in his warm breath on the back of my neck and his arm around my waist. Hungry for the closeness, I wriggled

175

further into his warmth. He tightened his grip and mumbled words that vibrated on my skin. A rogue tear rolled down my cheek – for losing my father or for finding myself. As I let sleep take me, I reckoned it was the latter.

"It's finished."

I lurched awake. Nethy was in the doorway holding the metal bottle in both hands high above his head as if he'd won a football match.

"What the – what's the time?"

"The sun is on its way down."

"How far on its way down?" Why didn't these people have clocks?

"It will be dark soon."

We'd slept the sleep of the gods. I shoved Burn. "Wake up."

Outside the house, Burn, Nethy, his wife, the girls, and a bunch of villagers encircled me. The bottle was heavier than it looked and I strained to hold it. "Nethy, thank you, but couldn't you have used a lighter metal?"

"Is there more than one?"

I groaned and glanced at Burn.

"Now what?" the gruff voice from the night before called.

"Now, we wait."

Everyone sat down, apart from Burn. I struggled over to him, trailing the bottle in the dirt. "What are they doing?"

"Waiting."

"For what?"

"The show."

I looked at all the expectant faces. "They really need a television. I'd bring one back with me but you don't have electricity."

"Are you coming back?"

"Oh." I propped the bottle against my legs. "Might do."

"You hate this planet."

Scratching my head, I said, "Not all of it."

"Which parts do you not hate?"

I squinted into the neck of the bottle. "We need a stopper."

"You are changing the subject. Which parts?"

"A strong one I'd say." I ran my finger around the opening.

"Edward!"

I faced him with square shoulders and chin jutting. "You. Okay? You. I'd come back to see you."

Burn flushed and his eyes glistened. "Really?"

"Yes. I've had heaps of friends, dated loads of girls and known countless bootlickers. But you are the only person who has ever been true and honest and seen the real me."

A tear rolled down his cheek followed by another.

"Oh, don't do that. You're still the most annoying person ever." I heaved the Collector catcher on to my shoulder and plodded away.

"Where are you going?" Burn called.

I stopped and shrugged. "Any suggestions?"

"We could wait by the river?"

"Okay. Come on."

I sat on the riverbank with the catcher between my knees, and Burn lay on his back pretending to smoke a pipe reed. The whole village gathered behind us. I flicked my thumb over my shoulder. "Why are they still here?" Burn didn't answer. "They really need WiFi or something."

"You do not have to do this, Edward."

"You've said that a hundred times."

"I do not think it is a hundred times, maybe two or three."

I sighed. "This will be the first time I've done something that will really make a difference, mean something, and leave my mark. You get me?"

"No."

An hour or two passed – time had no meaning any more. The Copper River glowed in the evening light and as the sun disappeared behind the horizon, the warmth went with it. "For God's sake, when the Collector's not welcome it bugs the life out of us, and when we want it there's not a tendril to be seen."

Burn sucked in his cheeks and took a long draw of his pipe.

"That's annoying."

He blew out nothing but fresh air. "I am bored."

"When I was a kid we used to light hollow grasses and smoke them.

It tasted disgusting. Have you ever smoked properly?"

"Yes. A roasted weed called jaracca."

"What does it do?"

Burn propped up on to his elbows. "I can show you."

"Eh?"

"Behind Nethy's forge is the perfect place for it to grow. There will be some there."

"Will I end up naked?"

"I cannot say."

"I don't know, Burn."

"Come on, it will relax you."

"I am relaxed."

Burn raised an eyebrow.

"Okay, okay."

We made our excuses and darted, as fast as the bottle would let me, behind the forge.

"What does it look like?"

"It has thin furry leaves."

I delved a hand into the thick foliage behind Nethy's hut. Something that felt like rat's tails brushed my skin. "Yuck. I've found it."

"Good." Burn's hands slid down my arms and his fingers enclosed mine. "Together. One. Two."

"Burn, I reckon I can pull a plant up."

"Not this plant. Pull."

We tugged as one. Nothing. We tightened our grip and heaved. The plant didn't budge. "What are its roots made of? Nethy's iron? Again."

Squeezing my eyes shut, I dug my heels in, readjusted my grip, and yanked the furry son of a Horeweevil for all I was worth.

"Edward, you're making too much noise."

"Noise?"

"Yes – grunts, puffs, and snorts. People will hear us."

"Are you worried about the fact we are pulling up jaracca or that they may think we're having sex?"

He giggled. "Oh, I would not worry about the latter." He slid his hands further down the plant and rumbled, "One more pull and that should do it."

"Well, I hope nobody overheard that."

We yanked, the plant released its grip on the earth, and we fell backwards into a tangled heap of limbs. I held the prize aloft. "I hope it's worth it."

In a wood clearing a short distance from the village, Burn roasted the leaves, hung like hunting trophies from a metal bar, over a fire pit. The bitter smell made my eyes water and my nostrils tickle. I did a full three-sixty turn – nothing but trees, the night, and unease in my bones. "Burn, why the secrecy? Are these leaves illegal?"

"No, not illegal. But it is considered bad-mannered."

"Are you being rude, Burn?"

"We both will be in a minute." He slid the leaves off the bar, on to a flat rock, and then pounded them with a stone. He delved into his leather bag, produced a small square of animal skin, and then he rolled the fragments into a tube.

"Here." He held it out.

"You first."

"No, it is always jaracca virgins first."

"You're making that up."

"Maybe."

I took the roll-up and placed it to my lips. Burn held a burning stick from the fire to the end. To look cool in front of him, I inhaled far too deeply. If burnt bodies tasted like anything, then it was this. Coughing and spluttering, I held the offending object at arm's length.

Burn pressed the roll-up back towards my mouth. "Try again."

"Have you got an ulterior motive for all this?" I searched his mind and frowned. "You're better at the door-shutting thing than me."

He laughed. "This trip has improved my telepathic skills."

I took a slow drag; the smoke singed a trail into my lungs, and my head spun. After the second drag, I had a strong urge to sit down and after the third, the world slowed to a crawl and pulling my knees up to my chest took too much time. I placed the roll-up to my lips again but Burn snatched it away.

"That's enough. Wait a few minutes and you will see why."

I backed up against a tree and tried to control my erratic breathing. Then a sudden awareness that I was a winged god hit me.

"Burn," I slurred, "you didn't tell me I was a divine being that was able to fly. You should've told me earlier, I could've flown away from the Collector." I tutted and shook my head. "That was a real oversight on your part."

Burn rolled on the red earth choking with laughter. "You are not a god," he spluttered.

"Oh, that's blasphemy. I am, too."

"Okay, do something god-like." Burn puffed on the remains of the roll-up.

I made to stand but my body was so heavy I couldn't move. "You're gonna have to lift me up so I can fly to the moon."

"The moon? We do not have a moon."

"Who's stolen your moon? Tell me and I will strike them down with my Spear of Destiny."

Burn crawled over and shoved himself between my legs. "Where is the spear?"

Now all I could see was the back of his head. "Hidden," I said to his hair.

"Where?"

I scrabbled around in my fuddled brain and found no answer. "It's a secret."

Burn rearranged my legs and sat in my lap with his knees either side of my waist. I allowed him without question. He leaned on my chest and puffed his jaracca-smelling breath in my face. "You can tell me."

His scrawny body was much heavier than it appeared. "Burn, you're squashing my wings."

Burn slipped a cold hand under my shirt and up to my shoulder blades. "You have not got any wings."

"Are you sure?"

He slipped the other hand up to join the first and stroked circles on my upper back. "Yes."

"Fucking hell, whoever has stolen the moon has also stolen my wings."

"It seems so. I am sorry."

I tried to focus on Burn's faces. "There are two of you."

"There are two of you as well." He settled his hands on my waist. "A foursome springs to mind."

"Oh, thanks, now your depraved image is in my head." I frowned. "Good God, there's far too many arms and legs thrashing around. You're sick."

"I feel sick."

"Yuck. Get off." I shoved him over.

He lay face down in the dirt and giggled. I chuckled. Then he snorted, puffing up red dust that made me bellow with laughter. Warmth puddled in my chest; he actually was good company. I fell sideways to join him, laced my fingers behind my head, and watched the stars disappear and re-appear in the swaying leafy canopy. "I'm hungry."

"Me too."

"Can't be arsed to get up."

"Me neither."

"I'm not a god, am I?"

Burn's hand slipped across my shoulders. "I do not think so."

"That's a shame," I murmured and closed my jaracca-heavy eyes.

"And!" Burn shouted. I opened one eye. "It seems we do have a moon!" Shafts of silvery light decorated his face.

"That's nice," I said and let sleep take me.

I awoke with my nerves on fire. It was still dark, but I knew the Collector was near.

Shaking Burn, I shouted into his ear, "Where's the bottle?"

He opened his eyes a fraction. "Um, what?"

"The bottle? Where's the fucking bottle?"

"Erm, still behind Nethy's forge."

I staggered to my feet, tottered towards the river, paused, spun round, stumbled back, and twirled on the spot like a ballerina. Fucking mind-altering leaves. "Burn, point me in the right direction." He pushed me through a gap in the trees and followed, looking over his shoulder.

"Where is it?" Burn said.

"It's here, I can sense it."

We found the catcher on its side behind the forge. I heaved it into my arms. "Quick, let's get to the river. Have you got the pipe reeds?"

Burn nodded. "Will it fall for the same trick twice?"

"Let's hope it has no ability to learn."

I dropped the bottle with a thud on to the riverbank. "Fuck, we never got a stopper for it." I whipped off my shirt, screwed up one end, and forced it into the neck. "That'll have to do." Burn handed me a reed as I moved to stand next to him. "Are you ready?"

"No."

"It'll be fine."

"You do not believe that."

Bloody telepath. "No, I don't, but it's the best plan we've got."

"We could run."

"And keep running? No. It needs stopping. Are you with me?"

"Of course, Edward."

I draped an arm around his shoulders as an eerie silence enveloped us. Burn stiffened, and the hairs stood up on the back of my neck. Ramming the pipe into my mouth, I dived into the river and submerged. Unlike before, I had no idea where the beast was since the water was as dark as the night. I swirled in the current and strained to see any shape that showed the Collector was above me. Nothing. As time passed, I drifted further away from Burn and the catcher. I resurfaced into the shadowy night. My stomach rolled over as I called for Burn and I swam to the bank. Silence.

I pelted back through thorny bushes to where I'd left him. "Burn," I bellowed for the tenth time.

I found him lying on the ground with foam bubbling out of his mouth, his limbs stiff and protruding, and convulsing like a toy soldier on a drum.

"Fucking hell, Burn." I dropped to his side and tried to hold him still. "Burn?"

Black wisps snaked out of his nostrils. For all that was holy, he'd inhaled the Collector alone and this time it was killing him. "No, you can't have him," I roared in my friend's face.

Without thinking, I clamped my mouth over Burn's and sucked. His body writhed under me as a charred taste filled my throat. My eyes bulged and my head throbbed in pain as I drew the Collector out of him. Oxygen left my body, replaced by the beast. I began to judder and with all the strength I could muster, I crawled over to the bottle. Death was beating at my door and weirdly, I was okay with that. Lugging the neck of the catcher to my mouth, I forced my lips over the end and blew, breathed in through my nose and I blew again. I exhaled until my face burned and fresh air rushed into my lungs. Then I forced my shirt back into the bottle's neck and flopped on to my side, panting.

"You kissed me," Burn's weak voice said.

"I did not, that was a, um, medical procedure," I puffed.

"It was a kiss."

I sat up and faced him. He'd drawn his knees up and his head was in his hands. "You okay?"

"I will survive. You?" he mumbled.

"I've had worse days."

Then a howling, as if we'd captured a hundred demons, came from the bottle as it bounced along the riverbank. I stood and took a few paces back. The trap spun on the spot as the wails increased. Burn joined me to witness the imprisoned Collector blow in fury. Then the bottle fell on to its side, rolled into the river and vanished under the dark water.

Burn shuffled to the water's edge. "Now what?"

Peering into the river I said, "We hope that's the end of it."

"We should wait."

"What for?"

"To make sure it is, um, dead."

"It's trapped in a metal bottle under the hated water. It'll be extinguished. Stop worrying." I took his shoulders and guided him away.

"You have done what you desired. We can be at your ship by sundown tomorrow," Burn muttered.

I coughed and massaged my shredded throat. "Finally." I had an overwhelming urge to weep. I'd avenged my father's death but felt no joy. Now all that was left to do was go home.

Chapter Sixteen

The sun was peering over the Copper River as we waved our goodbyes and set out along the bank. Nethy and his wife had stocked us with too much food and unnecessary blankets for a short walk, but for politeness' sake, we took them.

"What will be the first thing you do when you get home, Edward?"

"I've fantasised about a hot bath and eating the contents of the fridge, but that comes after visiting my mother's grave." I had missed her more on this trip than ever before – her tinkling laugh, her reassuring arms, and her faith in me. I took comfort in the fact that if there was an afterlife, she would be with my father now.

"I am sorry."

"Don't be. You understand what it's like to be an orphan."

"Yes, but I have had longer to come to terms with it."

"What are you going to do when I'm gone?"

"Nothing."

"Nothing?"

Burn looked at his feet as we walked. "I – do not know yet," he said to the ground.

I stopped and seized his arm. "Come with me."

A single tear rolled down his pale face. "I cannot."

"Why not?" I demanded. Burn was a link – to my father, to Abaytor, to a different me. I didn't want to lose that – or him.

"It is – complicated."

"Don't tell me you've got a secret wife and four children stashed away somewhere."

Burn fiddled with his fingers.

"You haven't?"

"No, I have not."

"Phew."

"Are you relieved, Edward Kemp?"

"No, no, no, I didn't say that."

"You didn't need to." He paused. "Believe me when I say I would love nothing more."

"Then come, Goddamn you."

He strode away and I had to jog to catch up. "You're so good at shutting mind doors."

"I felt you rooting around up there."

"Tell me, Burn."

"No."

"Tell me or – I'll knock you flat."

He stopped. "Edward, you are not quick enough for me."

I dropped my rucksack on to the ground with a thump and smiled at him. "Do you want to bet?"

Burn slowly slid off his bow, leather bag, and blanket roll, and then sprinted up the bank as if his arse was on fire.

I howled my version of a war cry and ran after him. He was fast, but I was now leaner and fitter, and could match him for speed. He veered to the right into a tight coppice. I followed him in, beating away the thin branches as they whipped my face and arms.

I spotted his copper hair darting through the trees. "You can't run forever," I called after him.

"I can run longer than you, alien boy," came the reply.

I swerved to the left. "You're the alien," I shouted.

Then he emerged from the right and ran in front of me, I pelted forwards and rugby-tackled him. We smacked the ground with a thud, both groaned in unison and sprawled face to face. "Got you," I panted.

"So it seems," he whispered.

We breathed each other's air for a long moment as Burn scratched around in my mind. "Hey, space invader, get out of there."

"You used to hate me invading your space."

"I still do."

Burn slid a free hand down my back and rested it on the waistband of my shorts. "Oh, I do not think so."

I bit my lip as a heat rose through my body. I stared at him. His eyes that were the same colour as the river, now had a blue tinge to the edges.

"Your eyes have changed colour."

Burn shifted his hips. "Edward, if you are trying to get into my trousers, that is a rubbish line."

I looked away. "No! I'm just saying that's all."

He giggled and his body shook under me. I dropped my forehead on to his and laughed with him.

Edward, you can get up now, my head said but I didn't want to move. Ever. And Burn knew it. He knew everything. He wriggled out of my hold and held out a long hand. I took it and he hauled me up.

I dusted down my battered shorts. "We better go and get our stuff."

We strolled in silence for a while, both lost in our own thoughts. The grassy path gave way to slabs of rock and, along with it, the river changed from a gentle gurgling flow to a wild abuser of anything that came in its way.

"We are not far now." Burn pointed. "Up ahead we will come to a precipice which overlooks the Plains."

I stopped and gushed, "One more night."

"What?"

"One more night," I repeated.

"Why?"

"Dunno."

"You do not know –"

"Forget it." I stalked off.

Burn caught my arm. "One more night, Edward."

I lay on my blanket with my hands behind my head gazing at a star nursery cluster. Burn lay next to me propped up on one elbow. "Remember me, Edward."

"Don't be so emotional, I'm coming back."

He said nothing.

"I'm coming back," I repeated and turned to face him.

"What will you do when you come back?"

"My father said the study of the bees had to be completed before he could implement the mass importation to Earth. I have no idea exactly what that means, but I intend to find out, and I can help with that."

That would be my duty but my selfish drive would be to see Burn again.

"You? Help with the studies?"

"Shut up. I could." I pushed him on the shoulder. "Also, we could fight monsters together."

"Monsters?"

"We'd be the *Men in Black*."

"Black?"

I shook my head. Being friends with Burn was like having an age gap relationship. My popular culture was not his popular culture, if in fact he had one. "The Bloom will not stay quiet for long."

"It is not your responsibility."

"It's not yours, either." I paused. "We could also hang out."

"Hang out?"

"Chill, unwind, shoot the breeze."

"No."

I groaned. "Spend time together."

In the light of the moon, Burn smiled. "Does Edward Kemp want to be my friend?"

"Edward Kemp *is* your friend."

Burn flopped back on to his blanket and rumbled a contented noise. "I win."

"Win?"

"I won you over."

I laughed. "Yes, you did."

"What is my prize, alien boy?" Burn asked as he wriggled over to my side.

"Not what you're hoping for, native."

"Oh, what is it then?"

I patted around and felt the strap of my rucksack. "I can offer you a top of the range Silverstrak with built-in music player," I said with a straight face.

"No, thank you."

"A used pair of Mika sneakers?"

"No."

"I have nothing else to offer." I smiled at him.

"Are you sure?"

"You're so fucking persistent."

He laughed and dropped his head next to mine. As Burn's breathing steadied, I closed my heavy lids.

A body, curled up in the corner of the crannog, his cries of fear echoing off the wooden walls. The room glowed with a blue light. Above the person hung a black cloud, shifting its shape from the vague to a winged beast and back again.

I strode right through the Collector, unaffected by its foul air, knelt by the man, and took his arm. "It's okay, you're safe with me." The figure unfurled and turned. I whimpered and staggered away.

I awoke, shaking.

"What is it?" Burn whispered.

"A dream."

"What about?"

"Something fearful."

"Forget it," Burn soothed. "Your dreams will stay on Abaytor."

I wasn't so sure.

My father's ship, alone and alien, sat in the centre of the barren plains.

"Well, there she is."

"She is small, no bigger than my house."

"She's not that small, there's sleeping quarters and a galley."

"What does the captain do all day on his own in the middle of nowhere?"

"My father set him environmental tests to do, and he has contact with Earth."

"How?"

"Through satellite communication."

"Satellite?"

"My father set one in orbit around Abaytor on his first trip."

"Orbit," Burn said slowly.

"Are you sure you don't fancy a ride to my planet?"

"I cannot, Edward." Burn sighed.

"I could teach you so much."

"What about?"

"Um, cars, phones, televisions, the Internet."

"Are those things important to you?"

Spending hours talking to strangers on the Internet and the rest of the time watching endless repeats on TV suddenly seemed so strange. "No, actually, no, they're not."

"I belong here." He set off down some natural worn steps. I hesitated and then followed.

The *Wave Rider* and all she stood for had been my aim for these godforsaken weeks. So why didn't I feel like celebrating?

She was the culmination of years of my father's life, and for such an important vessel, she had a rag-tag appearance. My father and his team had cobbled her together, like a huge metal Frankenstein's creature, from junkyard parts. The front didn't match the back and I'm sure there was a row of toasters welded to the side.

I glanced at Burn, then down at myself; dishevelled and skinny, we looked ready to drop. The profound silence between us was palpable. We had spoken little in the last hour or so.

"So what do you think?" I waved an arm towards the ship.

"It looks, um, intriguing."

"Do you want to look inside? Meet the captain?"

"No," he whispered.

"Why not?"

Burn shuffled his feet in the dirt.

Even though he'd shut his mind doors I knew something was wrong. "Burn? What is it?"

He scrubbed a mucky hand across his face. His long eyelashes were wet.

"Burn? You're making me nervous."

"It is time," he blurted.

"To go?"

"Yes." He paused and placed his hands on his head. "For you and for me."

"That's been the point of this whole journey."

"That is not what I am talking about, Edward, I am not really here," he said on a gush of air.

I frowned at him. "What do you mean, *I am not really here?*"

"The Bloom, um, revived me to, um, take you to the Basin."

"The Bloom? Revived you?"

"Yes."

"To take me to the Basin?"

"Yes."

"Fucking hell, Burn. What *are* you on about?"

"In exchange for my life, my job was to take you to them." A tear traced a clean line on his dirty face.

I curled my fists. "You. Fucking. Traitor."

"No, Edward. No!" Burn held up his hands to calm me. "It is not like that. I defied them. They thought I was weak but I fought them."

"Fought them?"

He sighed. "Yes, Edward. You are repeating everything I say. It is irritating."

"Welcome to my world. So you fought them. How? Mentally?"

"Yes."

"For all this time?"

"It has become easier as time has gone on."

"That's why the Collector never went for you."

Burn nodded and stared at his feet.

"So are you Burn or something else?"

"Every part of me is Burn." He lifted up his shirt and grinned. "Want a feel?"

"No! When did *it* happen?"

"When I had the encounter with the copper allagarta. I drowned in the river, and came to on the bank with the Bloom in my head shouting instructions."

"Instructions?"

"Repeating again."

"Sorry. You didn't think that it was important enough to tell me?"

"No."

"Why?"

He shrugged. "I could handle it and I did not think you would care."

"I would've."

"Back then?"

"Okay, maybe not." I bit my lip. "So you're a ghost?"

"Sort of."

"Sort of?"

"Edward!"

I turned away from him. He was *so* irritating. He couldn't be dead. His chest rose and fell. Surely, that meant life. "I can see you breathing," I said more to myself than to Burn.

Burn took my shoulders and spun me back round. He stepped towards me. His face was inches from mine. God. Damn. Ghostly. Space. Invader. He leaned in. I didn't lean back. He smelt of the river. "Yes, I breathe," he said, pursed his lips and blew softly on to my cheek. My skin prickled. His eyes searched mine for the answer to the only question he'd ever had. There was no sound except my heart clattering in my ears. I took a deep breath and whispered, "Damn it all to Hades."

I pressed my mouth to his and even though he was *sort of* dead, Burn's lips were warm and tasted of herbs. The kiss was for his companionship, his bravery and for *never* giving up on me. He quivered with surprise, emitted a low moan, and pressed his hands into my lower back dragging my body into him. His urgent searching lips forced my head back as he slid cold fingers under the waistband of my shorts.

I drew back, rested my forehead on his, and blew out a long breath that I hadn't realised I'd been holding. Dead or not, he was keen. "Whoa, how long have you wanted that?" I took a step away but made sure I was still in his space, and I smiled to myself – I'd kissed a boy and I'd liked it.

Burn paled even more. "Ever since you fell off the *Queen* in the Fire Glade," he murmured.

"I was horrid to you then."

"You are horrid to me now."

I opened my mouth to protest but Burn pressed a finger to my lips. "I loved your spirit. You were, and still are, new and intriguing. And alien. Who does not want to kiss an alien?" He flashed a smile and then dropped it as quick as it came. He took my hands in his and held them tight. "I have to go now, Edward."

"Go? Go where?"

"I managed to stay until I got you to the Landing Plains – which I have done. My time is up."

"NO!" I shouted. The protest surprised me.

Burn grinned in the lopsided way he does. "Does the famous Edward Kemp want me to stay?"

"Come with me," I mumbled.

"I am afraid I cannot."

It was not supposed to end like this. I was to get on the spaceship, not look back, and be happy to leave Abaytor, and my annoying native companion. But I wasn't happy. I was devastated. Turning from Burn I stared at the *Wave Rider*.

Then my hands felt so empty. I knew he'd gone.

There was no puff of smoke, no beam of white light, and no goodbye.

I fell to my knees, dropped my head on to the ground, and sobbed. Hot tears dotted the red dust as my world stopped spinning. I'd lost both my parents and now I'd lost my best friend.

A man's voice behind me said, "Sir. Are you okay? I've been waiting for you. Are you ready to board?"

I looked up into the confused face of my father's trusted pilot. "There must be some way on this weird and wonderful planet to get Burn back." I stood, wiping away my tears.

"Who, sir?"

"The Bloom will know."

"The Bloom?"

"Failing that, Naylor."

"Naylor?"

I smiled at the Captain and glanced at the *Wave Rider*. It had meant everything. Now, it meant nothing. I took a long stride in the opposite direction.

❖

About Michelle Peart

I am a writer, a designer, and a lover of the fantastical.

During the past two years, I have completed four writing courses, two at an advanced level, and passed all with Distinction.

To the Left of Your North Star is my debut novel.

Manifold Press

Life in all the colours of the rainbow

For Readers: LGBTQIA fiction and romance with strong storylines from acclaimed authors. A variety of intriguing locations - set in the past, present or future - sometimes with a supernatural twist. Our focus is always on the characters and the story.

For Authors: We are always happy to consider high-quality new projects from aspiring and established writers.

Our 'regular' novels are now joined by the Espresso Shots imprint for Novellas and our New Adult line.

Visit our website to discover more!

 ManifoldPress.co.uk